We Are The Old Souls

Ella Marshall

We Are The Old Souls

Ella Marshall

Text Copyright © 2023 by Ella Marshall
Cover Copyright © 2023 by Chloe Marshall

Published in Hillsborough, North Carolina

Paperback ISBN: 979-8-218-16420-1
Ebook ISBN: 979-8-218-16419-5

Library of Congress Number: 2023904462

First paperback edition June 2023

Edited by Ella Marshall and Jacqueline Marshall
Cover art by Chloe Marshall
Layout by Ella Marshall

Printed by IngramSpark

Dedicated to my family, both given and found. To my little sister and my mom and my dad. To my Aunt Sina and Aunt Lisa and Aunt Vicky and Aunt Crystal, to my uncles, Steve and Jon and Travis and Ethan. To my family, you've always been here for me, and I will never forget the support you've given me all my life. This book is dedicated to them, my very own old souls.

1

Aurora

When I was a kid, my mom always used to ask me what I wanted to do with my life. She used to ask all the time, from when my answer was to be 'a princess' to when my answer became an author.

Let's just say it was 'a princess' for a long time. Like much longer than I'd like to admit.

Of course, she sort of thought that they were the same thing, because 'an author isn't achievable, Aurora.' Her words, not mine.

But the jokes on her, I guess. She's the one paying for a fifty thousand dollar degree in English Literature.

But that's beyond the point. Growing up, there was always something I couldn't do. From riding my bike to swimming, there was always going to be something I wasn't good at. Not that I ever accepted that— I never have and I never will.

But hey, I got into Weston University, so there's that. And with a scholarship, nonetheless.

That has to say something about me, right?

So here I am, too young to make a good pot of pasta but old enough to pack up all of my things and move halfway across the state. Southport is only three hours away from Durham, (four on a bad day) but I'm allowed to exaggerate. My head is pounding with pain as my brother whistles along to the mindless music playing through the radio. Thankfully my mom isn't reading her guide books anymore— they made her too nauseous so she's taken an impressive amount of NyQuil and passed out in the backseat of my *brother's* beat up Chevy. It contrasts heavily with his looks, but I'm not sure he cares anymore. A few years ago he was the type of guy to wear beat-up paint covered blue jeans, but not anymore. Two years ago he detested doing laundry so much he'd wear his shirts inside out instead of washing them. Now he's obsessive when it comes to the state of his perfectly-starched khakis and button down shirts. He's gone from the guy you'd spot doing keg stands in the backyard of some rent house to the guy who'd persecute keg-standers for underage drinking. The only thing that's stayed the same since he left for college is his hair. It's stayed a floppy black mop that hangs in his eyes more often than not. Even his eyes have changed a bit over the years. What were pale brown irises in a wide-set eye have become dark and thin, encumbered by stress and covered up by thick tortoise shell glasses with fake lenses.

"You're nervous." He guesses on the first try, knowing me well. Caleb and I have always been close, in spite of the three-year age gap. He was fourteen when our dad left, so he had to step up a lot more than a boy his age should have had to. I've always considered him my closest friend— which is really just sad, if I'm being honest.

"Of course I am." I snipe at him. I barely catch him rolling his eyes out of the corner of my own, and he chortles at me as he receives a slap to the arm. The glasses that are far too large for his face slide down his nose a little bit, weighed down by their gigantic frames. He started wearing false glasses after high school— he says they make him look more professional— though I haven't been able to get used to the gigantic glasses in the years since they entered our family.

"I'm sure you'll do great, Rora."

"Of course I will. But I'm still freaked out about it." I insist. Caleb always has been a bit over protective. Especially since Dad left; he really had to step into the role of being the protective father figure.

It's honestly a bit messed up.

"Well I'm always a call away. I'm headed up to New York for a couple months in December for my internship but other than that, I promise I'll be right here."

"You don't have to take care of me. I'll be fine." I insist. I know Caleb better than I know the back of my hand, and no matter how much he annoys me sometimes, I love him more than anything. He's always been here for me, and some part of me knows I'll always be indebted to him.

"Sure you will, Rora. But I'm allowed to be worried. I watched you nearly catch your cereal on fire this morning." You may be wondering how in the hell that's even possible, and honestly, I'd tell you if I knew. However, I don't think I ever will. I'm the most impressively unimpressive cook in the world, according to my ever-so-kind mother. If it comes from the kitchen, I've caught it on fire at some point or another. Quesadillas, grilled cheeses, pasta, veggies, a salad at one point, cereal, and a hell of a lot more.

"There's a cafeteria." I state as though it's the most obvious answer, and he rolls his eyes. The tortoise shell frames hide the movement ever so slightly when they catch a beam of sunlight—which, of course, is directed into my eyes as he moves to get away from the blinding sunlight. I can't help but wonder if he'd notice if I just slapped them off his face.

They're really not doing him any favors. For a six-foot-tall ex football player with the sharpest chin you'll ever see, you'd think he'd realize that covering up part of his face isn't making him any more attractive.

"I know that." He sighs. I choose to believe it's an admission of guilt when it comes to the stupid glasses, but alas, it is not. Of all my brother's uncanny abilities, reading my mind has never been one of them. "I still worry. Just be careful. Don't die, alright?" And with that, he allows me to go back to my reading. It's a typical, cliché enemies to lovers book— one that I could swear I've read a thousand times over. I love it even more every single time, though. I have about thirty of them sitting in a box in the bed of the truck, each one dog-eared and messed up. I'm sure any librarian would have my head if they saw the condition of my favorite books. I choose to believe it isn't my fault, though. I just enjoy them too much; they've all been read over and over and over again.

I've always had a soft spot for clichés.

After several snack breaks and bathroom stops— and my mother throwing up in the back seat once —we finally make it to Durham just in time to see the sun go down from the tiny painted-shut window of our hotel room. A peeling no-smoking sticker is stuck to the window, and someone's drawn a penis over the cigarette. The smoke has been drawn into splatters of *you-know-what,* and I can't help but giggle as I pull my phone out of my back pocket— which is far too small for the large phone, resulting in it constantly falling out onto the floor when I sit down— and snap a quick picture.

"Aurora, honey, go get my medicine baggie from the car, I have a headache." My mother orders basically as soon as we're all settled in the hotel room and I've kicked off my shoes, forcing me to shut my book and rush out of the room. I'm already in my pajamas, which makes it rather awkward to walk down the halls. I feel as though I'm getting strange looks from others in the hallway as I go, though I return them with smiles. It's probably just in my head.

It definitely is. I'm in a fucking hotel, for petes sake.

It's warmer than I think it should be outside, but it is summer so I'm not sure why I expected it not to be. At home it usually cools down a bit and starts storming around this time, but since we're not by the coast I suppose I'll have to get used to different weather. I quickly unlock the doors to my brother's car, grabbing my mother's sparkly golden bag from the backseat. The pills shake and rattle as I shove the baggie under my arm and turn to shut the heavy rusted door. Suddenly, the air around me lights up and a bright, bright light hits my eyes. If I'm being a bit overzealous, I could call it blinding… but, in reality it's only a pair of headlights pulling into the spot beside me. Shaking, I grab my own bag of toiletries from one of the plastic totes in the flat-bed, remembering that I need it, and lock the doors again before heading back inside.

Okay, so maybe I'm a teeny tiny itsy bitsy little bit dramatic. It's not a big deal, though.

Naturally, by the time I get back to the room, my mother is already passed out cold on the bed, snoring away and my brother is channel surfing on the small, box shaped TV. The chainsaw sound emitting from my mother's throat has me flinching for a moment before it stops briefly and my brother looks over at her to make sure she's still breathing. Finally, after she begins snoring again, he looks back to the TV. It's the sort you would see in a cartoon, which is ironic given that he seems to have settled on an old episode of Tom and Jerry.

"Took ya' long enough." He grumbles, barely sparing me a glance as I walk into the bathroom to get ready for bed. I brush my teeth as fast as I can (which is absolutely nowhere close to the recommended time of two minutes), exhaustion catching up with me quickly after the long trip. My dentist doesn't like me very much, but he loves my brother, whose fancy electric toothbrush sits in an equally fancy travel case beside the bed. Fishing a melatonin tablet from my bag and tying my hair back in a pair of dark brown braids which fall down to just below my shoulder blades, I collapse into the bed beside my mom. Surprisingly, for the first time in longer than I'd like to admit, my eyes drift shut and I'm fast asleep within minutes.

～ ☾ ～

Fire burns all around me, licking at my skin and singeing the unshaven hairs on my bare legs. I know I should run, but my mind goes blank as I see my father standing there amongst the chaos just a few feet in front of me. He looks like a devil amongst the flames of hell, though he's always looked that way to me— like Lucifer, beautiful on the outside but rotten on the inside. He is the personification of evil.

"Hello Aurora, long time no see. You could have visited."

"Leave me alone." I shout. I've been having these nightmares for years, every time something good happens in my life. Caleb still talks to our father often. In fact, he's got an internship at his company in New York this winter. It's something I've always felt guilty about, not being able to forgive him for leaving our mother six years ago. That and the fact that he's never once done anything more than send a card for any important event in my life.

When I was fourteen and my appendix burst, he sent me a get well soon card that wasn't signed.

When I turned sixteen, I got a barbie card that wasn't even signed, as well as a gift card to some random clothing store that made me feel like shit just to enter.

And of course, a couple months ago when I turned eighteen, I got another card, this one with a picture of a 17 candle on the front. At least he signed that one, though. You'd think that would be the bare minimum amount of effort for a father to put into his

daughter's life, but even that has always been a stretch for my
sperm donor.

Anxiety smacks me in the gut as I'm pulled away from the
dream.

~ (~

Much to my relief, I wake up pretty quickly, breathing heavily with exertion. My heart beat is loud in my head and there's a heavy layer of sweat covering my face and arms. Pushing the covers off, I make my way to the smoker's lounge outside, standing on the empty balcony and swaying through a blood rush. I don't smoke, it's a habit I never cared to pick up, but the fresh air is exactly what I need after a nightmare. That or an antacid, both are acceptable in times like these.

"You okay?" Someone asks from across the concrete slab, making me whirl around. There's an older woman standing there with a half burned cigarette between her fingers, dressed in an old fashioned nightgown and slippers.

"Uh, yeah, I'm alright. Thanks." I answer quickly. I've never been good at talking to people I don't know, something that Caleb has never had a problem with. The woman sends me a raised brow but doesn't mention the clear awkwardness surrounding me.

"You look like you've just seen a ghost."

"No no, nothing like that, just a nightmare." I explain fruitlessly. The woman lets out a shrill laugh at the explanation.

"Want a smoke? It'll help with the nerves." She offers me the pack of cigarettes. Before I can think better of it, I grab one from the flimsy box, placing it between my lips. My brother used to smoke all the time, but when he was seventeen his best friend made him quit. He said it would ruin his life, and at the time I thought he was crazy for standing up to my brother. Not anymore. The woman lets out another deep laugh as she strikes a match on the wooden balcony, placing it a little too close to my face for comfort to light the stick of death hanging lazily from my lips. "Now inhale, stupid." She tells me when I sit there a little too long, trying to figure out whether to take a small breath or a big one— or hell, maybe I should just make a run for it.

I take a long drag off the cigarette, or at least, that's what I intended to do. Instead, I end up coughing up a lung. Figuratively speaking, of course. The woman laughs dryly as she watches me beat at my chest, trying to get the smoke to clear from my lungs.

"At least you gave it a shot." She says, taking the cigarette from me before I can light my hair on fire. The beautiful braids I'd placed in my hair a few hours ago are gone and replaced with a rats-nest. One ponytail holder is gone and lost to the sheets in the dingy hotel room, and the other is barely holding on. I must have been moving a lot in my sleep. "Maybe you should stick to Tylenol, kid."

"I could have—" I begin, considering taking the cigarette back, but before I can she places it between her yellow-stained teeth.

"Nope, you don't need to get addicted to this shit, it'll make your life hell." She interrupts, taking a draw of the cigarette I had just been holding and replacing her own finished one with it.

"Then why did you give it to me?"

"Because you're young. Even old souls have to pretend to be young at some point."

"What does that have to do with anything?"

"Figure it out yourself, kid." She answers, and with that she puts out the cigarette and walks off back inside of the hotel, leaving behind a small box of matches on the wood beside me.

~ ☾ ~

I wake up the next morning on the ground beside my mother's bed, clearly having rolled off in the middle of the night — something I used to do often when I was younger. The shower is running in the bathroom and Caleb's bed is empty, whilst my mother is still dead asleep. Walking over to my bag, I grab hold of a pair of jeans and a t-shirt that I'm fairly positive I stole from Caleb, as well as a fresh pair of underpants and a bra that is two sizes too small for me, thanks to my insistent dislike of bra shopping with my mother. It's far too awkward for my taste, and she always manages to slip in a few rude comments. I glance at the tan cotton underwear for just a moment, briefly wishing that somehow my vagina weren't acidic and I had bought new panties to bring with me.

The jeans I had gotten on a whim when I went shopping with my one and only friend from High School, Gemma. They're the only fancy jeans I own, with holes around the knees that make Caleb laugh. He always asks if I had to pay extra for the holes, which always results in a slap to the back of the head for him. Stripping out of my worn out pajama pants and sweaty tank top, I quickly change into my clothes for the day and begin to pack up the items scattered around the hotel from the night before. It's around eight a.m. and my student orientation starts in two and a half hours, meaning we really have to get moving if we want breakfast on the way— which I desperately do.

Within an hour, we're out the door on the way to the closest cafe, a cute little one on the outskirts of Durham. My mother is still grumbling complaints about her lack of sleep from the night, so I make my way to the counter quickly, getting her a plain black coffee and three creamers, just how she likes it.

I can't stand plain coffee and cream, unlike the woman who birthed me. I have to have copious amounts of sugar to so much as swallow the stuff. The man working behind the counter gives me a curious glance before handing over the coffee and creamer and handing me back my card, which I happily stick back in the wallet stuck to the back of my cell phone.

I hate using a purse. Like, I vehemently hate it. With the passion of a thousand suns or something like that— I just hate it.

My mother drinks her coffee quickly while I eat my biscuit and drink my own, and soon enough, we're back on the way to the campus, everything piled in the back and ready to go. Boxes upon boxes and bags of clothing, all ready to be moved into a dorm room. I can't help but be excited for my future in college.

At least, that's what I'd like to think as my fingers find the box of matches in my pocket. The matches that remind me of the most interesting thing I've done in years and the feeling of adrenaline coursing through my body when it backfired on me.

I can't help but want to do it again.

2

Eric

*O*rientation is probably the most boring thing one could

ever have to go through. The explanations of this building and
that, the rules for campus life that I'm sure most break on the
daily. I'm not sure why they even bother to explain 'trash
courtesy', which is really just their way of saying 'don't get
caught littering'. It's the same as it is every year, and I hate that
we have to go through it every summer.

Of course, I say that like I've been here for years and years.
In fact, it's only been three, but it's torture nonetheless.
Especially with the volunteer's shrill tone as she explains yet
another donated park bench— spoiler alert, it's the same donated

park bench that's been there since I was a freshman. Peggy's bench. Someone's written KISSING in bold capital letters between the words.

I'm really regretting signing up for the early morning orientation. I'd much prefer to be back in my new apartment, which I'm sharing with my best friend, but instead I'm here.

It's not like I didn't spend the entire summer with him, anyway. Like I've been doing every year since we were ten. His family and mine have always been close, especially since his dad left a few years back. We were fourteen, and I know it took a huge toll on him. Not to mention that he basically became a father to his little sister. He's gotten more and more protective of her over the years.

Probably because she's gotten hot. What used to be a short and thin little girl with hair that was always messily chopped to chin-length has become something much more. She's grown of course, in more ways than one. She grew out her hair so it lies down on her back and she dresses a lot better than she did when we were little. She started to dress just like her brother did around the time we left for college— oversized t-shirts, baggy jeans usually covered in paint, and a torn-up book always sticking out of her purse or the pocket of her jacket. All she's missing is the red letterman jacket he wore every day through high school. Over the summer, though, she was beautiful. Pale crop tops she stole from her friends, jeans with massive holes at the knees that showed off a good amount of her tanned skin. If she were anyone else…

I shake the thought off as soon as it comes to me. I remember when we were younger, when she used to hang around us all of the time. It used to annoy the shit out of him, but once his dad left, he got all of the responsibility. Scaring away boys, making sure she was well taken care of, tucking her in at night and keeping the bullies away from her at school. He did it all, especially when his mom would go on work trips or ignore her for some reason or another. There was always a reason for Grace to ignore her youngest child; something she had done wrong.

"Any questions?" The volunteer finally asks, dismissing us only moments later. I love Weston, I really do, but they could do a better job with orientations. I can see the look on some of the freshman's faces saying they didn't get any real information out of that while several others rush over to the table to get their complementary rape whistle, which as it has every year, will have to be taken up after a few days because all of the frats will collect them and use them to announce pledge week.

Finally, as I make my way back over to my car, I catch sight of a head of floppy dark brown hair being pushed out of the way of too-large tortoise shell glasses that I'd recognize anywhere. Caleb turns around just in time as I nearly barrel into him, patting him on the back violently the way we always have.

"What the hell are you doing here, man?"

"Dropping off some of Rora's stuff while she's in her orientation." He answers as though it's obvious. Naturally, he forgot to tell me something important. He always forgets to tell me something important. You'd think that the years of business school would make him a little better at this stuff, but it has yet to make a difference. The only change its caused is in his wardrobe. He used to dress a lot more casually, but now he brushes off the arms of his baby blue button-down shirt once I've finished hugging him. To finalize my point, he finishes the action by pushing his massive and unnecessary glasses up his long thin nose.

"Aurora is going here? To Weston?"

"Yeah, didn't I mention that?"

"No." I answer, running a hand through my hair nervously. I know what he's about to ask me to do. It's the same thing he had me do in high school. It's something I've never liked to do.

"Well watch out for her, will ya? She's a bit fragile right now, I caught her having a nightmare last night. I mean— I'm close by, which is good, but I want to make sure she doesn't get herself into too much trouble. You know how she is."

"Sure, of course." I answer immediately, no matter how much I don't want to. I know how much trouble Aurora can get herself into, Caleb and I have had to clean up after her more than enough times for it to be drilled into my head. It's annoying to think about exactly how much trouble she could get herself into just by walking out her front door in the morning. She doesn't really like to think rationally, something that I'm sure is great for her writing, just not so great for… everything else. The number of parties I've stopped her from going to and people I've stopped her from talking with is insane. Caleb and I used to take shifts sometimes, one of us beating up whichever jack-off was all over her and the other driving her home and taking care of her in whatever state she was in. Thankfully, she never liked alcohol very much, only ever going as far as a few cups of cheap beer or a glass of rosé.

"Wanna help me move some of this stuff to her dorm?"

"Sure." I still have boxes piled up in our apartment and in the back of my car, but he gives me that look that always makes my excuses crumble. With that one glance we're off through the halls, both carrying a couple of boxes. Mine is heavy, and I can tell immediately that it's her collection of books. Funny enough, Aurora has a very specific taste in books, despite loving to write basically everything she can. I know by heart the books I'm shuttling up the stairs are a large collection of sappy, cliché filled romance books about a girl who falls for someone she's not supposed to. Each and every one of them has a hundred sticky notes stuck between the pages and several dog-ears on the pages she likes to go back and read. These are the books she hides under the bed and carries around in her pockets as a pick-me-up.

She loves them far too much for my taste, but whatever makes her happy.

I've caught her crying over them before. Like full on ugly crying. If I weren't so annoyed by the blatant lies she feeds herself through these books, I would have probably cracked up laughing.

We make it to Wren Hall pretty quickly and find our way to dorm 13A pretty quickly, opening the door and dropping the load of boxes in the empty bedroom. It's a bigger dorm than I had in my first year, this one having two separate single rooms off of a small hallway as well as a tiny sitting area and a couple of shelves for books and trinkets. One bedroom is already filled to the brim with belongings, meaning her roommate is already here. I can tell Caleb wants to snoop around— see who his little sister is going to be living with— so I grab his arm and tug him back out of the room before he gets the chance.

I'd like to say that the James family isn't irritatingly wealthy — wealthy enough to get their daughter into the most expensive dorm building at Weston, wealthy enough to basically pay for a two-bedroom apartment with two and a half bathrooms for their son to share with his best friend. Mr. James, their father, is the most awful, rude man you'll ever meet but you couldn't say he isn't good at making money. Not to mention his affinity for throwing money at his problems— sorry, children. He abandoned them years ago and hasn't bothered going back to

Southport ever since, but he sends cards filled with cash every year for birthdays and holidays.

We make three more trips before Caleb drags us across the campus to where Aurora's orientation was meant to end. We find her sitting on a park bench with her mother, who looks exhausted, bickering away about something or other like they do so often. Caleb rushes forward immediately whilst I trail behind him awkwardly. "Look who I found." He says, pointing to me. Aurora's gaze trails up from her brother to me, dark brown eyes going slightly wider than normal. If I didn't know any better I'd think they were gonna pop out. She's always been doe-eyed, with round eyes and thick brown lashes which surround even darker irises. They're beautiful. They both got their eyes from their father, which makes it that much worse that they're so pretty.

"I thought you were meeting at the apartment?" She asks, sounding startled.

"We were, but *someone* forgot to tell me you were attending Weston." I explain, sending her brother a glare. She gives me a tight lipped smile, standing awkwardly in front of me. I don't know whether to give her a hug or get us moving back to her dorm, so I give her an awkward pat on the arm, which I instantly begin to regret. "Let's get you back to your dorm, kiddo."

"I'm only three years younger than you, jerk." She insists, sticking her tongue out at me, sort of defeating her own point. I hold up my hands in mock defeat, letting her and Caleb walk ahead together. *Two and a half, actually.*

Aurora seems to pale a bit as we walk through the campus, clearly a bit overwhelmed by the size of it all. We made it to her dorm slower than normal, though she had to stop a few times to look at something interesting.

Of course, most wouldn't find a large oak tree particularly interesting, but she seemed to think it was the most magnificent thing in the world.

Aurora has always amazed me a bit, like a phenomenon no one can quite explain. She's always been so bright and happy, despite all of the terrible things she's been through. I'm sure the last three years have been awful for her, with how often her mom is gone and without her brother around to help out. She seems a bit different than she did the last time I really talked to her.

And with how often her fingers twitch, a sure fire sign that she's anxious. Aurora has suffered from anxiety since she was little, something she confided in me when I found her in an empty hallway at school once. I remember how scared I was, watching tears stream down her face as she tugged her legs close to her chest. I thought something terrible had happened, and I'm sure it did, she just never told me what exactly caused the panic attack that day. Ever since then, she's been a little bit distant with me though.

And she was always a bit of a strange girl, with her love of obscure animals and her fixation on princesses. She didn't get along with many kids her age when we were in school, similar to myself, but she never got to reap the benefits of having a socialite for a best friend. I'm sure my life would have been a lot different without Caleb in it, but she never really got the benefit of having him with her all of the time. She was in a different grade, isolated from him for a long time and when we got into high school, he was always off at football practices and such. We both played, so Aurora would sit in the bleachers and watch our practices quite often. At least, until the last quarter of our junior year.

I'm not sure why she stopped, though I've found myself wondering a few times. I've always figured it was because Caleb told her not to, but I have a feeling I'm wrong.

Aurora lets out a slight squeal as she walks into her dorm room for the first time. I remember when I did, too, although I wasn't as excited as she seems to be. She looks as though she's at the world's largest surprise party, all for her as she twirls around in the tight hallway. Caleb lets out a surprised laugh as she pulls him into a bone-crushing hug before taking off down to the sitting room, then into her bedroom. It's minimally furnished and barely large enough for all of us to stand in at once, but she looks like she's in paradise the entire time as she looks through drawers and checks for space in her closet.

Finally, once she's finished looking around, she opens up one of her boxes and pulls out a lamp covered in shells. I recognize it immediately, as it's been in her bedroom since she was a toddler. I'm sure it's been there longer, but that's the earliest I can remember. I was around five when I met the family, though I didn't get close with Caleb until years later.

As soon as she's finished plugging in the small light fixture and placing it on her bed stand, she sits down on the edge of her bare mattress, which seems as though it's been through a lot, but I don't bother to mention the disrepair. She looks so happy in the tiny little bedroom, I couldn't say anything to ruin it if I wanted to, and I really don't.

It's been a long time since I was around Aurora for this long at once. Since we were in high school, I'm sure, but probably even before that. It's always been Caleb I was close with, probably because of the age difference and the whole 'girls have cooties' thing, but now that I'm really looking at her, I can't help but smile at seeing her so happy. She was always just flitting on the edge of excitement growing up. Like a fire someone kept blowing on in an attempt to put out. Turns out, it was just oxygenating her, turning her into a blaze of happiness.

Caleb and I are kicked out of the room pretty soon after so that, in his mother's words, 'the ladies can unpack.' So we end up sitting in the bare sitting room and waiting for them to finish unloading the six boxes and a couple of bags. While they're doing this, we hear a loud shriek. Caleb jumps to his feet immediately, whirling around whilst I look to the door, finding a girl who can't be more than five-foot-three standing there, her pink hair peeking out of a towel and her t-shirt and shorts sticking to her still damp skin.

"What the hell?!" She shouts dramatically, giving us a confused look.

"We're with Aurora." Caleb stumbles over his words as she responds. The pink haired girl pushes the door to his sister's room open quickly.

"You've got two guys out here?! I could barely get my brothers to carry a box up here!" She says and we can see her tug Aurora into a hug in the doorway. She lets out a confused noise as she hugs the girl back, giving us a pleading look. "I'm Diana, but I go by Dee. You?" She asks chipperly.

"Aurora, Aurora James, it's nice to meet you." Aurora says politely. "And this is my brother Caleb and his friend Eric…"

"Honey, we are going to have so much fun… ooh! Are you unpacking? Can I help?" She asks, rushing into Aurora's room, quickly followed by the girl herself.

And once again, we're left to our own devices in the sitting room.

"So when do you leave for your internship?" I ask curiously, peeling my eyes away from the door Aurora had disappeared through.

What is wrong with me? Why am I looking at her like this? Why am I looking at her at all?

But before he can answer, Aurora is back in the room, yanking him off the couch and into her dorm room to show off. I trail behind him with a small smile, watching her grin forming on the bright expanse of her face.

The smell of apples and peppermint hits me like a train as soon as I enter the room. A smell I didn't know I enjoyed.

And there she is, sitting on top of her green comforter and holding onto a teddy bear I know my mom gave her four years ago when she got her appendix removed.

And that's when I realized it. She's wearing a shirt with a squiggly smiley face on it, a logo for a band that I know my best friend borderline despises. A band I've always loved.

She's wearing my shirt.

3

Aurora

$\mathcal{D}$ee and I end up decorating the sitting room together with

a bunch of colored paper, making makeshift wallpaper on one wall and adding a colorful blanket to the disgustingly stained couch. There are two windows on one wall— which we throw open —and Dee puts a couple of plants in the corner. It's small and modest, but I love it. Caleb and Eric left to sit outside a while back, claiming that it was too crowded in here while my mom went to look at lunch options for us, leaving me alone to get to know my eccentric roommate.

"So, you and that guy? What's his name, Eric?" Dee questions me, giving a small smile as she hands me another plant to put on the windowsill. All of the pots she has them in are painted with a bunch of different colors, so many it makes my heart speed up a tiny bit. I've always loved things that are so colorful it almost hurts, and I'm so glad Dee thinks the same way. This room will be amazing to write in.

"What about us?"

"Are you together?" She asks as though it's obvious, and it probably would have been had I been paying attention to the look she was giving me. A smirk and a single raised brow, like she knew something I didn't.

"What? No, of course not." I stutter out. I used to have a bit of a crush on Eric when I was a kid, but I got over it when he left for college. I had forgotten he went to Weston, of course, so him being here is a bit of a surprise to me.

"Yeah? Well the way you were blushing I figured you were trying to figure out when you could jump his bones." Dee says absentmindedly, straightening out a paper on the wall whilst I choke on my own spit.

"What? No! You can have him if you want, I'm not… you know."

"Honey, he isn't really my type. He's not a she." Dee chokes out through a laugh as my cheeks go even redder than before. She grabs my arm to keep me from turning away, though. "I was just curious, no need to be embarrassed. He's cute is all, figured you might be together."

"Well we aren't, I'm not really Eric's type either."

"I'm not sure if I believe that, but alright. Let's get going, I'm sure your moms' found something to eat by now."

~ (~

We end up at a small diner Eric recommended, one that seems to be straight from the fifties or sixties; Candy's. There are servers with pin up curls and checkered skirts that fall down to just below their knees— a couple even wear roller skates. There's even a jukebox on one wall and a small area for dancing, though no one seems to be doing so.

"What do you think of Weston so far, Rora?" My brother asks as he sips on his bottle of IPA, the same as Eric's. They've always tended to have similar taste in almost everything, so it's not much of a surprise they'd like the same drinks— even if it's the same bread-juice. Eric takes a long sip of his beer, Adam's apple bobbing as he swallows it down. He rests his chin on his hand, the stubble on his chin making an appearance with a passing shadow. His blonde hair is shiny beneath the sunshine from the window and his lanky arms are folded uncomfortably on the vinyl table. A gleaming watch rests on his left hand and there's a tattoo just further up his arm, black ink swirling into a cloud on his forearm.

"It's beautiful. I'm excited for classes to start."

"What are you majoring in? Do you know yet?" Dee asks curiously as she riffles through her pockets for something or other.

"Yeah, a double major actually. Literature and archaeology."

"Cool, I'm in fashion development. Eric? Caleb?"

"Caleb 's in business, I'm in anthropology with a minor in photography." Eric answers immediately. Dee nudges me immediately in the ribs, giving me a sly smile, much to the confusion of my brother.

We eat in near silence, much to my relief. I need some time to sort through my thoughts, but with Dee giving me strange looks every few minutes, it's a bit difficult.

By the time we're done eating, it's past two and Eric, Caleb and my mother load up in their cars and head back to the guys' apartment, leaving us to our own devices to walk back to the dorms. As we walk, Dee winds her arm through mine and steers me off to a small shop with a bunch of trinkets, not bothering to say much of anything as she looks around. They've got hundreds of prints and different jewelry and pottery, plus more than one crazy little statue. Finally, my eye catches on something I wasn't quite expecting to find here. There, in the corner of the room is a small plastic flamingo, the same as the ones that decorate my yard back at home, and nearly every yard in Southport.

And without having to think about it, I grab the flamingo and take it right up to the front of the shop. The owner gives me a strange glance as I purchase the flamingo, but she doesn't say anything about it as she hands me the bag.

Dee doesn't question the new addition to one of her flower pots, either.

~ (~

I wake up early the next morning, more so than I meant to, but that doesn't really matter. Grabbing my notebook and laptop, along with my cell phone and a few pens, I make my way out of the dorm quietly. I find myself at the large oak tree I found yesterday within minutes, cutting through the grass to get to it. Finally, I hoist myself onto one of the branches, smiling as I manage to sit perfectly balanced on the branch with my back against the trunk. It's more comfortable than I thought it would be.

So I pull out my laptop and I open up a new document. The words flow out faster than I can process them and my fingers dart over the keyboard faster than normal. It's like the words explode out of me and onto the untitled document, and I find myself writing page after page after page without pause, even as my fingers cramp up uncomfortably and my neck begins to ache.

It's a style of writing I haven't been able to do before, and I can't help but love it. I'm just so overwhelmed here, there are so many thoughts to get down.

And with that, I'm lost to a world of my own imagination. A world with dragons and assassins and shoes made of glass and a strong heroine unafraid to call out her love interest for his extreme level of stupidity.

"Watch it!" Someone shouts, startling me out of my daze with a rude awakening. Before I can even register it, a football smacks against the tree where my face was only a second ago, forcing a scream from my throat. Glancing up, I find three well built guys running towards me at top speed. "Are you alright?" The one with black hair asks, standing on his tiptoes to be level with my face. Glancing down, I find that he has eyes the color of coal and a single dimple on the left side of his face.

"Yeah, yeah I'm fine." I stutter out. I'll admit it, this man is gorgeous. I just can't help but stare at him a bit.

"Well that's good, wouldn't want hurting a pretty girl on my conscience, not sure I could handle it." He jokes, making a chuckle bubble up in my throat and a blush rise to my cheeks at being called pretty. I'm almost disgusted by it. Before I can say anything else, though, my phone begins to blare Starships by Nicki Minaj, much to the enjoyment of the man. I picked it up immediately, recognizing the ringtone as my brother's. "Caleb?"

"Where are you? I thought we had lunch plans." He says, clearly a bit annoyed. I can hear my mother in the background complaining. Pulling the phone away from my face, I can feel my eyes go wide at the sight of the time. I've been out here since seven in the morning.

It's twelve thirty now.

I let out a quiet curse at the sight and make a fast excuse, telling my brother I'd be there in a second before hanging up and closing my laptop.

"Everything alright?" The dark haired man asks me curiously, watching me try to figure out how to get down.

"I'm late for lunch." I explain. He takes the laptop from me quickly, setting it down before grabbing my hips and pulling me down from the branch gently. Of course, it gets a bit awkward when I stumble right into his chest. I'd call it cutesy but it really isn't, it's just sad.

"Come on, I'll walk you." He says, grabbing my laptop and notebook once he's sure I'm stable on the ground. He leads me over to the sidewalk quickly, letting his friends know he'd be back soon before we begin walking to my dorm. "I'm Gray, by the way. And you are?"

"Aurora, Aurora James." I answer awkwardly, a blush rising to my face as he tugs me out of the way of an oncoming skateboarder.

"A bit of a walking disaster, aren't you Aurora? Is this your first year?"

"Yeah, I just moved in yesterday." I explain. I'm not offended at being called a 'walking disaster' the way I used to be when Caleb and Eric called me things like that. From Gray, it almost seems endearing. That's probably a weird thing to say, though.

"Nice, I'm a sophomore. Are you from around here?"

"The coast, actually. You?"

"Virginia. My dad is in the military so I grew up on base with him and my Mom."

"My dad was a marine before he and my mom had my brother." I find myself confiding in him. I can't help but like Gray, he seems so kind. Of course, I know there's a chance he could be a jerk, but I feel like it's worth talking to him a bit.

"That's cool." Gray says as we walk up to the building my dorm is in, finding Caleb and my mom sitting on a bench together. Caleb stands as soon as he catches sight of me walking up with Gray, immediately grabbing my arm and tugging me next to him.

"Who's this, Aurora?" He asks, his scary big brother voice coming out.

"This is Gray, we met at the tree I found yesterday."

"My friends nearly hit her in the face with a football so I figured it was the least I could do to walk her back. I'm Gray, Gray Anderson, and you are?" He asks, holding out his hand to shake Caleb's.

"Caleb, Caleb Murtery." He says, shaking Gray's hand firmly. If he notices that we don't have the same last name, he doesn't mention it, only moves on to my mother.

"Grace James, it's nice to meet you but we'd better go, we have a reservation." She says politely. Gray nods and hands me my things before walking away.

It's only then that I notice a small slip of card-stock hanging out of my journal. A business card.

Grayson Anderson
Greenscape Newspaper
Editor

909-973-2027

A small smile rises to my face as I read it over, but I allow Caleb to lead me to the car without saying anything.

Off to another boring lunch, I suppose. But this time, at least I have something to be excited about. I'm not sure why I'm so excited at getting a guy's number, but it's nice to have a friend at Weston. At least, a friend who isn't forced to spend time with me like Eric and Dee are. I like them, of course, but it's nice to feel as liked as I do right now.

Sometimes I wonder if it's normal to feel the way I do all of the time. To question people as much as I do or to get so exhausted so often. I know I shouldn't be questioning it, at least, that's what Dr. Mitchell tries to get me not to do. He thinks it isn't good for me to think about whether my anxiety is normal or not.

We end up at a different restaurant than the one we went to yesterday, sitting in the corner of the room as my brother grills me about Gray.

How did I meet him?

Did he and his friends hurt me?

Why did I let him walk me back to the dorm?

Do I realize that he knows where I live now?

Am I really that stupid?

Every once in a while, I despise my brother for being so protective. I know he does it to keep me safe, I swear I do, but he makes me feel so completely idiotic sometimes. It feels like he thinks I'm a child still, like I'm the same twelve year old he had to hold every night to get to sleep.

But I'm not.

4

Aurora

$\mathcal{P}$ulling on a pair of jeans and a green, tight t-shirt that I know makes my pale skin look good, I can't help but be nervous for my first day of classes.

I've got three today, and I'm terrified to say the least. I shouldn't be, I mean, I've been preparing for this for as long as I can remember, but I'm still scared. Grabbing my small, gray bag and my textbooks and notebooks, as well as my laptop, I make my way out of the dorm and lock the door behind me.

I wish I could just stay there, but I know I can't. Instead, I make my way through the campus to the mathematics building for my first class, grabbing a coffee from the cart on the way in.

The man gives me a strange look as he sees me pour seven packs of sugar and four pods of creamer into the dark liquid, but he doesn't say anything.

Finally, I find myself in a room filled with people, all with notebooks and laptops out, ready to take notes. Quietly, I take a seat in the middle of the room, placing my coffee on the table in front of me and pulling out my laptop and a notebook, which I've already labeled for this class. The teacher walks in pretty soon after that, just as I finish my coffee and she begins the lesson.

I hate statistics. I always have, since we started learning about it in middle school. I remember how Caleb was always really good at it. He was amazing, actually. And he loved the bragging rights he got when he helped me with my homework, my messier scrawl clear as day against his perfect cursive. I'm sure my teachers hated it, but none of them ever said anything as long as I did the work too.

An hour and a half feels longer than it ever has before, but the class finally finishes up around noon. I've already got a page and a half of notes, and it's only the first day. I knew college was going to be hard, but I'm starting to think I'm going to need another notebook if I'm going to make it through this class.

I make my way to the cafeteria after that, starving already since I didn't eat breakfast. The room itself is huge and filled to the brim with wooden tables. The ceiling is probably the highest

I've ever seen and there are rows after rows of students sitting and studying or chatting amongst themselves. Quickly, I make my way to the line and grab a bag of chips and a pre-made peanut butter and jelly. Finally, swiping my card, I'm able to get out of the crowded cafeteria.

As soon as I get to the door, I see my tree. I know exactly where I want to go.

~ (~

Sitting in my tree with a book in one hand and my sandwich in the other, I'm happier than I have been since I left for lunch yesterday.

"Mind if I sit with you?" Gray asks, startling me out of my thoughts as he silently sits at the base of the tree, holding his own sandwich.

"Hey, sure. Of course." I stutter, giving him a small smile and setting my book over my thigh to keep the page I was on.

"Your brother seems nice." He says absentmindedly, digging into his turkey and cheese.

"If by nice you mean overly protective and rude, then yes. He was a bit much, I'm sorry about that."

"It's alright, I understand. His sister showed up with a guy he'd never met, he was a little freaked out. I'd be the same way if it were my sister." He tells me, sending me a small smile to tell me he's serious and it's alright. I let out a small breath of relief at the knowledge.

"You have a sister?"

"Yeah, but she's four. Won't be bringing guys around for a while, I hope." We both laugh at this. He hands me a bottle of water kindly as I finish off my sandwich and climb down to sit next to him, offering him a chip from my bag, which he happily accepts. "Thanks."

"Of course." I say, leaning my head back on the trunk of the tree.

"So what's with you and this tree? Secretly a tree hugger?" He asks jokingly, gently nudging my shoulder with his.

"No, I just like it. It's a pretty tree, and it must have been around for a while to get this big."

"I imagine so. We could cut it down and count the rings."

"I don't think the school would appreciate that much, and to be fair, neither would I. I'm happy having it stay a mystery, I just like the thought." I explain with a smile, offering him another chip as I continue to sip on my water.

"Fine, I won't cut down your tree…"

"Good, I'm glad I've convinced you."

"…if you go on a date with me this weekend. Saturday night, dinner and a walk around campus?" He offers up. A blush rises to my cheeks and taints my neck and ears as I choke on my water, barely avoiding spraying it out of my nose.

Sputtering, I beat on my chest as I choke, coughing the way I did when I took a breath of that smoke a few nights back. Like I'm hacking up a lung. I'm sure it isn't the most attractive thing I could do in response to being asked out for the first time.

"Okay, so maybe not the best time to ask, I will take that into account. *Do not ask a girl out on a date while she's mid-sip.*" He says, miming making a check mark and laughing as he pats my back lightly. "You okay?"

"Yeah, sorry, I'm alright." I say, chuckling slightly at his joke. "Sure, that sounds great. I'll text you and we can go over details, alright?"

"Alright then." He says, standing up and walking away, leaving me there at the base of a tree. I can't help but squeal inwardly at the thought of what had just happened, dialing the only number in my phone I could ever think of telling about this sort of thing. If I were in a romance novel like the one currently sticking out of my jacket pocket, I would be doing mental somersaults through the grass.

Who am I kidding? I am doing mental somersaults through the grass. Actually, I'm doing mental back handsprings through the grass and leaping over pedestrians like an olympic gymnast.

~ ⟨ ~

The hall I'm in is huge, larger than I expected as I put my phone back in my pocket and make my way to the front of the room, taking a seat a few rows from where the teacher is meant to sit.

This teacher is younger than the statistics teacher, with bushy brown hair and a slightly unbuttoned shirt. He looks to be in his late twenties or early thirties. He's got round glasses and a five o'clock shadow as well.

"My name is Dr. Stephen Genesis, I'll be your Psych 101 professor." He says, voice booming through the microphone system. "Raise your hand if you're majoring or you think you'll major in psych. Any form, go on." He says. A bunch of hands raise up around me, though I'm sure half of them only want to please the man. He raises a brow at the sight of those of us without hands raised lowering in our seats, embarrassed at not being one of the people he's called out. There are only about twenty of us in the group. "Alright, lower your hands. This'll do. Who can tell me what psychology is?"

Hands go up everywhere, everyone knows the answer. Even so, I lower myself in my seat, unsure of my answer. I know I should raise my hand, tell him I know, but I don't. My mind races to find the dictionary answer, but I can't.

Stupid anxiety, filling my head with bees.

"You don't know, Miss…?" He asks, pointing to me. I want to vomit.

"James, Aurora James. It's the study of how our minds work, sir. How they function and affect our behaviors."

"And you didn't raise your hand because?"

"Because I wasn't sure."

"Good. You've done it right. Everything you assume you know about psychology unless taught to you by a professional, you can assume is wrong." He says. "Assumptions are never completely correct. Good job Aurora, don't assume you know things when you don't. And to those of you who want to study psychology, you should know that every mind is different. We all think differently, feel differently. No-one is the same as any other, we're all unique."

~ ☾ ~

After two hours of having our brains smashed by Doctor Genesis, we're finally let go. I make my way to my next class quickly, smiling at passersby as brightly as I can after a long day. My head hurts already and I'm still reeling from the exchange with my psychology professor.

I make it to my classroom quickly, thankfully, and without interruption. This room is smaller, though I can already see Dee's pink hair in the midst of the tightly-packed crowd. Quickly, I make my way down to sit with her, pulling out my laptop and preparing to focus on the class I already know will be my favorite.

"How's your day been?" Dee asks me quietly as people shuffle for seats around us.

"Pretty good, but my psych teacher made a demonstration out of me, which was awkward." I explain, giving her a small smile.

"That sucks."

"But I got asked out on a date!" I tell her, suddenly remembering the good news I was planning to share with her. She squeals out excitedly, grabbing my hand and shaking me slightly.

"Oh my god! What's his name? Can I help you get ready? Oh, this is so exciting!" She says happily.

"His name is Gray, yes you can help me get ready. It's Saturday, but that's all I know right now. I'm gonna text him later to find out more."

"Is he cute?"

"Yes, extremely. I'm just worried Caleb'll find out and drive him away. He's so gorgeous and so nice, and he's the first guy who's ever actually asked me out." I confide, running a hand through my tangled hair.

"We'll make sure he doesn't find out, it'll be fine. Caleb isn't your father, he can't pick who you date."

"If it were up to him, I'd be sharing an apartment with him and wearing a potato sack to class every day."

"Well I won't let that happen, honey. Caleb won't find out about your date, just you, Gray and I will know, promise."

"Thanks Dee," I say.

And then the professor walks in, and I recognize her immediately. It's the woman from the hotel, the one who gave me a cigarette and a cryptic message.

How very odd.

5

Aurora

*F*aster than I'd like to think is possible, Friday comes

around and Dee drags me out shopping as soon as her class is
finished. I didn't have one this morning, so I got to sleep in—
something I'm exceedingly thankful for.

"So, what are we thinking? Jeans and a cute shirt? Sundress?
Fancy dress?" She asks as she rifles through the racks at the
small boutique we're at.

"We're going to the diner we went to the other day and then
we're going on a walk around campus, so I think jeans or a
sundress. Nothing too fancy." I say, looking through the racks

myself. Countless dresses and none that catch my eye, making it an annoyingly fruitless and long trip.

Finally, I come across the one I like. It's a maxi sundress with a cutout, tied together around the stomach like a top and a skirt held together with strings. It's beautiful, really, with one sleeve that goes over the left shoulder and a deep back.

"That's pretty, are you gonna try it on?" Dee asks me as I take it off the rack. It's a beautiful shade of red, but the material is light and flows like a sundress. It's the kind of dress that can either be fancy or understated, depending on what you wear with it. Sort of like me.

"Yeah, I think so." I say, checking the size to make sure it'll fit. It's a medium, so it should be fine, especially with how stretchy the top is.

I love it.

I nearly jog to the fitting room, shutting the door behind me as fast as I can and peeling off my jeans and the nirvana t-shirt I stole from Caleb. The dress fits perfectly over my breasts and pools around my ankles, meaning I'll have to wear some taller shoes to keep it from dragging on the ground, but overall I love it. It's a beautiful shade that compliments my skin well and really brings out the red in my hair.

So I pull open the door. Dee lets out a squeal as she sees me, smiling brightly at the sight of me in the dress. I wish I knew what she's thinking as she grabs my hands and makes me twirl around so she can see the dress in all its glory. "You look beautiful, Aurora." She says before shooing me back into the dressing room to take it off and get dressed again.

I hate to take it off and put back on the boring pants and oversized t-shirt, but before I can get too sad I'm reminded that I'll be wearing it tomorrow on my date with Gray.

And nothing can ruin how amazing that feels to know.

We purchase the dress quickly, both giddy with the feeling of having bought such a beautiful thing. We make our way out of the shop, arms intertwined as we rush through the town together.

We walk along the sidewalk slowly moments later, enjoying our walk and reveling in the success of our quest to purchase the perfect dress. Suddenly, my eyes catch on the most beautiful little park I've ever seen, with swings and a small slide and bench. I grab Dee's hand without thinking, yanking her towards the swings.

I swing higher and higher, as high as I possibly can, listening intently to the sound of my new friend's laughs as she too pumps her legs to swing. It's the type of thing I used to love to do as a child, and now that I'm an adult, it's just as fun.

"I like you, Aurora. You're a good person." Dee tells me as we walk back to the dorms together later that night.

"I like you too Dee. What brought this on?"

"I don't know, I've just never really met someone like you before. You're different than I expected you to be. When my mom was in college, her first roommate was some kind of crazy evil bitch. I sort of expected that."

"Just wait until you find me crying in the sitting room one night, you won't be as impressed with me anymore." I tell her, coaxing a small giggle from her lips. Dee is one of the nicest people I've ever met, I'll admit it. She's sweet and I've gotten used to her company over the last week. She's even started trying to convince me to dye my hair purple or something to match hers.

Something my brother would flip out about, by the way.

"Thanks Dee."

"Of course, now. Tomorrow at five-thirty is your reservation right?"

"Yeah, that's what Gray said."

"Good, that'll give us plenty of time to get you ready and to sleep in a bit. We could even go get coffee in the morning if you'd like."

"That sounds great."

~ ☾ ~

I end up in bed fairly early, surprising myself when I fall asleep easily, swaddled in my green comforter and matching sheets.

I wake to the feeling of the bed beside me bouncing, making my head bounce against my pillow. Peeling my eyes open, I find

Dee sitting on the edge of my bed, holding onto my shoulders and bouncing on the mattress to wake me up.

"What the hell, Dee?" I whine as I force myself to sit up, shaking out of her hold.

"It's noon, come on, let's go get coffee." She says through a giggle, pulling me out of bed quickly and shoving me in the first thing she can find in my drawers, a pair of jean shorts and an outer banks shirt I purchased at some random shop a few years ago. It's a bit small on me now, but it'll do.

We make our way down the street together after only a few moments, finding the first coffee place we see and grabbing a couple of drinks.

Dee gets some sort of special, chocolate infused coffee.

I get the sugariest thing on the menu, a caramel flavored latte drink. I've never had it before, but the second the caramel touches my tongue, I know I'll love it. The sweet mixture of caramel and coffee works well and I wolf down the whole drink within minutes before tossing my cup and letting my roommate drag me over to the grocery store before we head back to the dorm.

My roommate paints my face with a random assortment of items, keeping the look light but beautiful at the same time. She's an artist when it comes to makeup, apparently, and I love the result more than I've ever loved anything I did myself.

Finally, with my lips painted a pale pink and my eyelids shaded with silver and gray, I strip off my shirt and pants and pull on the dress. I pick out some silver, slightly heeled sandals to go with it.

~ ☾ ~

Five o'clock; Dee leaves the dorm and tells me she won't be back for a while.

Five thirty; the reservation passes and I get a call from the restaurant. They've called him ten times and have resulted to calling the secondary contact he left— me.

Six o'clock; I'm starting to worry as I call Gray once, then twice.

Six thirty; I've been stood up, haven't I?

Two hours, several unanswered calls and a bit of crying later, I do the thing I didn't want to do. I start to panic.

My breath comes faster than normal and my heartbeat speeds up. My palms begin to sweat and my vision goes blurry with tears.

Maybe he's sick and he just forgot to call or something. I try to think— try to allow the thoughts to sink in, though they remain floating just above the anxiety, barely out of my reach. He isn't sick, he just stood me up, and that's obvious.

Dee left hours ago for her own date, one with a girl named Maddy she met in town a few days ago. She's going bowling, and of course, here I am without anything to do but panic.

After a moment, I make the decision— probably a stupid one — to call my brother. The phone rings three times before he picks up, much to my relief.

"Caleb's phone." The deep tone of my brother's best friend fills my ears, though his words don't come close to sinking in.

"C, it's happening again. You told me to call—"

"Aurora, take a deep breath. Caleb left for the bar an hour ago and forgot his phone. Are you having a panic attack?" He questions, though the thought alone of telling Eric that I'm freaking out… let alone that I've been stood up by someone my brother didn't even know I was going out with— I'd rather just deal with it myself.

After a moment of silence, I shut the phone off, ignoring the small pool of guilt that forms in my stomach as I toss it on the bed and take a seat on the rough, carpeted floor.

My breathing comes fast and hard as it leaves my lungs, feeling as though it's raking up my esophagus with nails like knives, leaving behind stinging pain in its wake. Within seconds I've managed to lay down on the hard floor, letting the rough carpet that I'm sure hasn't been cleaned in years scratch against my face painfully. I hate this feeling— the feeling of utter and complete uselessness that comes over me when this happens. It's as if everything I've ever done no longer matters and I'm defined by the anxiety that seems to be always rushing through my veins.

That isn't important, though. What's important is that nagging feeling in the back of my mind that says that I deserve everything that's happened to me. That voice that tells me that because I'm so fucked up, I deserve every last second of misery this world sends my way. I despise it like nothing else.

I don't know how long it takes for the feeling to begin to fade, for the tears to begin to stem and the pain in my chest to begin to disperse through my fingertips and leave my body like a ghost inhabiting my very skin and bones. I don't bother to stand as it goes away, making me feel as if it wasn't ever really there. The only remnant of that pain is the feeling of tiredness still in me and the feeling of self hatred.

After a moment, the door pops open and someone speaks softly to the person with the key— probably an RA.

"Is she alright?" The woman questions, though the other person simply shushes her.

"It's an anxiety attack, she'll be alright." It's Eric, I know that. I just vaguely remember him asking if I was okay a few moments back, though I don't really remember much else from the conversation. Just hanging up on him. I remember that part and my cheeks warm slightly as I feel the weight of his hands settle on me. He lifts me into the air for only a moment, his chest pressing against my face for a second before I'm swallowed in my comforter. He tucks me under the fabric quickly before taking a seat beside me, making the bed dip at my waist.

"Talk to me, Aurora. Tell me you're alright." He says as though it makes sense to be frantic right now. Perhaps it does, though I can't see a reason for him to care so much. Eric is a lot of things, but a man who cares isn't one of them. He doesn't play the comfort game, he plays the pat you on the back and pretend nothing's happening game.

"I'm fine." I say simply, though my voice betrays me, coming out raspy and quiet. My lips are too dry for comfort and my eyes are stinging from the tears, though the feeling isn't foreign to me. It's annoying, but it isn't foreign. "I'm fine."

"You didn't sound fine on the phone. I would have gotten Caleb but he's all the way in Hillsborough for the night, 'said he'd be hanging out with some friends from his stats class."

"I don't want him to know." I say before I can think better of it, knowing full well that Caleb will freak out if he knows I was going out with a guy, let alone one he didn't know that well.

Especially since he stood me up.

He stood me up.

6

Eric

"Mason! Mason!" I shout loudly, knocking on the boy's

door with both fists. The door flies open a moment later, making me nearly fall through, though Mason catches my fists before I can hit him in the chest.

"What's your problem, man?" He asks, though I know I didn't wake him up since it's so early. His TV is playing quietly in his room and he's got a bunch of notecards abandoned on his floor.

"I need you to open up room 13A." I breathe out quickly, earning a chuckle from the man.

"I'm not trying to lose my free housing, letting you into a girl's room. What're you so freaked out about?"

"You can come with me or something, I just need to get to her. She called me freaking out, I swear man I got here as quick as I could. My roommate's in Hillsborough for the night and she tried to call him, it's just-."

"Calm down, man, calm down. I'll call Daisy, she'll let you in. She's the female RA, I'm just not allowed to let you in myself since I'm a dude." He says, walking back into his room and dialing a number on the cord-phone on his dresser. The person picks up almost immediately and he explains the situation fairly quickly before hanging up and pulling on a pair of shoes. "Come on, we'll meet her on floor A and she'll let you in. I'm coming with you, don't want you getting lost."

"Thank you, Mason."

~ (~

Daisy gives me an odd look as we stop in front of room 13A, the only one on the hall not decorated with white boards and stickers and names written in cursive on slips of paper and notecards.

"I'm gonna be honest, I thought this room was empty. I've never seen anyone coming in or out and they haven't gotten any complaints from the other girls."

"Aurora isn't big on partying, you wouldn't have come across her."

"Okay." She says awkwardly, finding the key on her keychain amongst around 50 others and unlocking the door to the suite I was in only a few days ago.

I walk in ahead of her, calling Dee's name a few times before shoving the door to Aurora's room open. She's laying on the floor and there are fresh tears on her face, though she isn't actively shaking or anything. Her eyes are open, though she doesn't move and she looks as though she's seen a ghost.

"Is she alright?" Daisy questions, though I shush her immediately, watching the girl on the ground not so much as flinch.

"It's an anxiety attack, she'll be alright." I whisper, wishing more than anything I could believe it. I find myself picking her up under the arms and legs, cradling her to my chest for a fleeting Moment before placing her on the small, twin sized bed. Her green comforter billows under her, so I pull it from beneath her legs and place it up to her neck, figuring she'll be cold. Finally, without a better option, I take a seat beside her.

"Talk to me, Rora. Tell me you're alright." I beg, knowing from Caleb just how these panic attacks can leave her— in bad shape.

"I'm fine." She tells me, her voice raspy and painful-sounding. It's as if she's speaking for the first time in weeks.

"You didn't sound fine on the phone. I would have gotten Caleb but he's all the way in Hillsborough for the night, said he'd be hanging out with some friends from his stats class—"

"I don't want him to know."

That's new.

"Okay… he doesn't have to know, just tell me how I can help."

"Just… stay, for a bit? Please?" She asks, almost begging as she shuts her eyes. I know she isn't asleep yet, but with every second I can feel her muscles losing their tension and her face resting its features. Within a few moments, she's nodding off and soft breaths are leaving her lips, a hundred times more even than they were just a moment earlier.

Part of me wants to pull her close, but I don't. I stand up, grabbing a pillow from the side of the bed where she'd kicked it off and a blanket from the stack of partially folded ones at her feet, the ones she uses for decoration. Without thinking, I place a kiss on the top of her head and I place the items on the rough carpet floor, laying my head on the pillow and putting the blanket over my legs— it doesn't cover my head, as it's fairly short.

~ ☾ ~

I don't manage to sleep for very long as the door slams open and Dee's voice fills the small dorm.

"Rory! How'd the date go?!" She shouts, walking past the door as I stand up, walking out into the hall and shutting the door behind me.

"*Shh.*" I shush her, making her jump and turn around, one hand still holding up her left foot, midway through unbuckling her heel.

"What are you doing here? Where's Aurora?" She questions, yanking the heel off and tossing it into her bedroom.

"She had a panic attack. What date?"

Dee stays silent, her cheeks flushing as she battles with her brain over whether to tell me or not. "Tell me, now. I found her freaking the fuck out three hours ago, don't test me right now."

"She had a date with that guy she met, Gray. He was supposed to pick her up at five. She wasn't meant to get home till after eight; what do you mean you got here three hours ago?"

"Yeah, well, clearly something was lost in communication." I say, running a hand through my hair in frustration. *Of course it was over a guy. That's why she didn't want Caleb to know, he'd be freaking out by now.* "Just… stop yelling, okay? I'm gonna go back in there."

"Fine." She says, almost begrudgingly but there's something in her eyes that makes me think she's happy about this. Leaving her behind in the tiny sitting room of their dorm, I make my way back into Aurora's room, only to find her sitting up against the bed frame with her back against the wall and a painfully sad look in her eyes.

"She told you." It isn't a question. She already knows the answer well; she knows I know what caused all of this.

"You should have told Caleb, if only to be safe. Or even me, for that matter." I explain, taking a seat beside her. My feet hang far off the bed, more so than hers do, but the second her head falls against my arm I know I don't care about the small discomfort.

"I know. I just— he's just—." She starts a few times, losing the sentence part way through every time. She doesn't know what to say anymore, I know that. I know the feeling.

"He's protective."

A small sigh leaves her chapped lips, though she's clearly not as upset as she was before. "Exactly. He would have tried to drive him away or lock me up in your apartment or something."

"I know. Caleb is a lot of things but subtle isn't one of them, sadly. Do you wanna tell me what happened? He didn't hurt you, did he?"

"He stood me up." She says simply, tucking her face a little further into my arm to hide her reddening cheeks. I don't know why the anger seems to fill me at the thought of her sitting here, waiting for a guy that'll never show up, but the thought alone makes my fists ball up uncomfortably.

"Oh." I say, not knowing what else could help her through this. Before I can think better of the ideas popping through my head, I stand up, knowing that this will either mess everything up or make my life a hell of a lot better. "Come on, we're going out."

"Eric, we-."

"I'll wait in the hall, go get dressed, alright?" I ask before she can say anything. Her eyes light up a tiny little bit for some reason or another as she scurries into the other room, her footsteps heavy with excitement.

I make my way out to the hall quickly, watching for a moment as she rushes around in Dee's room, the startled girl rushing around with her in search of something or another.

My palms run over my jeans several times, the nerves I feel making themselves apparent as I wait for her for a good thirty minutes. I can hear her inside getting ready, yelling at Dee to grab this or that from her room. Her roommate is clearly excited, her happy giggles filling the room every once in a while when Aurora says something she deems to be entertaining. I can't help but be glad the pair are getting along so well. My roommate freshman year was a jerk, to say the least. Always smoking in the dorm— which is very much against the rules —and playing his music too loud for anyone's taste besides his own. I'm sure our RA hated us.

~ ☾ ~

She appears after a bit, her frame clad in bright red and her eyes shining with something along the lines of excitement. She's an inch or two taller than normal thanks to a pair of strappy silver heels and her cheeks are flushed with a false blush that makes her red-brown hair stand out perfectly. She looks beautiful, like an angel sent to make my stomach stir in a way I couldn't have expected to feel.

"You look—"

"I know, I'm sorry. I tried to be fast so it doesn't look so great."

"Beautiful. You look beautiful, Aurora."

"Thank you." She says, cheeks darkening a bit with a real blush that sits just underneath the false one.

"Shall we?" I ask, offering her my arm. I feel woefully underdressed compared to the beauty beside me, but I couldn't care less with the way she relies on my arm for balance. The only imperfections are the small bags beneath her eyes, a reminder of the man she was meant to be going out with tonight.

But she's with me. Me.

Caleb would be peeved with me if he found out about this. He would probably punch me, if I'm being honest, but I can't help not caring.

"Where are we going?" She asks as I shove the heavy metal door of the dorm building open in front of us, welcoming the cooling air into my lungs with a feeling alike to bliss. Part of me wishes I could see her smile and twirl around the way she did when we got to her dorm for the first time, but she stays stuck to my side, clearly not wanting to run around. Not when she was just stood up and certainly not with the pain of it still ever-present in her brain. Half of me wants to think that she's doing it to be close to me, but I know she needs comfort and that's all she wants with this. She doesn't want me close, she just wants someone close.

That's what I have to believe. *This is no big deal, just me helping Caleb's sister. This is what he asked me to do.*

But deep inside, I know I'm lying to myself. She's so beautiful, more so than I could have ever thought she would become when we were younger.

"Wherever you want to go."

"The park?" She asks hopefully, a small smile on her face. I'm not sure what park or where, but the small lights coming on in her eyes make my brain feel fuzzy, and I know that right now, I'd follow her all the way back home if that's what she wanted me to do.

I'd do just about anything she wanted me to do right now, and I have no idea why, but I know I'm fucking screwed if I let it continue.

7

Aurora

My dress crumples slightly under my thighs as I push
myself to slide down the green plastic slide, halting a few times
and feeling the burn of the sun-burnt plastic underneath me, but I
couldn't care less about the small sting as Eric lifts me up from
the end of the slide, setting me on my feet again. He lets me go
as soon as I'm upright and stable, though my mind wanders to
the romanticism of the books I read that tell me he should be
spinning me around in a circle or holding me close to his chest.
Though if that were the case, my dress wouldn't be wrinkled and
ruined to the point that I'm sure it's going to take a millennia to
get all of the mulch out of it, but the smile that graces his face as

I pull him towards the swings is more than worth it, even if it's not like in the books. He's different than I used to think he was, with the easy smile and bright eyes that never used to adorn his features. In fact, it's probably the happiest I've seen him in a long time, since before he went to high school, at the very least.

He takes a seat on the swing beside me, large hands finding the chains that hold him up as he swings his legs gently to get going, toes scraping the mulch-covered ground with nearly every swing.

"So… what's his name?" He asks after a moment, his smile shrinking a bit as he asks the one inevitable question. The one I knew he would ask eventually, though I suppose midnight in an abandoned park isn't the worst time to have what is no doubt going to be a horrid conversation.

"Grayson. His name is Grayson."

"Anderson?"

"Yeah." I say, not even noticing his apprehension till he forces me to see it. He curses under his breath, hand coming out to snatch the chain of my swing, pulling me out of my movement and to a wobbling stop.

"Don't go talking to Gray Anderson again, Aurora." He warns, and I'm sure I would mistake it for a threat if it weren't for the look in his eyes, the look that says that he just wants the best for me, whatever that is. "Trust me on this, he isn't a good guy. He's a gossip freak that likes to cause trouble with everyone he can. He's even got instagram gossip pages up everywhere, if you know where to look."

"…okay." I say after a second, watching as relief fills his eyes. "Is it terrible that I want to believe that he just lost track of time?"

"No, Aurora. No it's not bad, it's just not what happened, sadly. He's just an ass, nothing more. This isn't like the books you read, he just isn't a good guy."

"I wish it were like the books." I admit after a moment, staring intently at my hands clenched together in my lap in order to avoid his eyes. I know he's confused, maybe a bit worried, but I can't help the words falling from my lips. I trust Eric, I really do, I just don't want to see the look on his face right now. Not really, not at all.

"What do you mean by that, Aurora?"

"I wish I could imagine this all away. I wish I could live another life, without all of this shit that's happened. I just… wish I could change it. I wish I could find someone and have that cliché romance and I wish that all of this had never happened."

"All of what?"

"Everything. Ever since Dad left, everything's gone to shit for me. Then Caleb left and you left and… everything just slowed down. It was like everything around me was moving and I was just… still. I don't want to be still anymore, Eric. I can't stand it."

"I know. You always were an old soul, Rora. I know that house was always hell-on-earth for you."

"You say that like it wasn't your own personal hell too."

~ ☾ ~

Eric's arms wrap around my waist tightly as I bury my face in his chest, knowing I'll have to let go in a moment. He doesn't show an indication of wanting that any more than I do, and I can tell he's a bit disappointed when I pull away and walk back into my dorm. Dee's light is off and her soft snores fill the air as I pull off my dress and take a washcloth to my face, washing away any remnants of makeup and tears still there after the long night I've had. It's at least one in the morning by now, and I know I won't be waking up till the afternoon if I have the choice.

I find myself in bed within a few minutes, my body tucked under the sheets and blankets. My eyes beg to flutter closed, but my brain moves too fast to let them.

But just as I'm about to give up, my phone dings beside me.

Sleep well, Aurora. Let me know if you need anything.

I know the text is from him. It's obvious, actually. It has to be from him. Before I know what I'm doing, I'm pulling up a new contact and placing a photo I snapped of him earlier in the picture slot. His eyes are bright with happiness and there's a small smile on his face, highlighting his perfect dimples with ease. He's truly a statue of human flesh, perfection as a human being. Finally, I place his name in the contact and press okay, permanently remembering this night in the form of a contact with my brother's best friend's name on it. I most definitely shouldn't have done that.

~ ☾ ~

"Come on, come on!" Dee shouts at me as she yanks me through the aisles of the Walgreens, looking for the perfect shade of purple to dye my hair. They've only got like five boxes but she's insistent we find just the right one to make my hair look perfect against my quickly paling skin. It's been a while since I was in the sun as much as I used to be, so the tan I garnered over the years has become a simple glow on my skin. I don't hate it, no, but I do miss the warmth of the tan I had gotten so used to throughout my life in Southport. Even during the cool winters, the sun was bright and it made my skin continuously tanned— and often burned as well.

She finally decides on a deep plum bottle of semi-permanent dye to lather in my pale brown hair. Making our way back to the dorms, she drags me to the communal showers with dye and plastic gloves and a plain white t-shirt in hand, as well as a bright pink shower cap with the word DIVA spelled out in sparkling cursive letters on the back.

"Just the ends, right?" I question as she lathers purple dye into my hair, never getting too close to my scalp for comfort, though I still can't help but worry. Neither of us can afford getting our hair done professionally, given the whole 'broke college student' thing, and I'm still not sure how I feel about entrusting my hair to an 18-year-old girl with the most raging case of ADHD you'll ever see.

"Yes, just the ends. Chill out and relax, it's like a spa." Dee chides, tugging slightly on my hair to get her point across. Not nearly hard enough to be painful but just enough to annoy me slightly.

"Okay then, as long as you're sure."

"I am, now shut up and relax."

And I do, and my hair ends up being a dark shade of purple that blends in well with the pale brown of my hair.

"I told you you'd love it." She insists, chuckling as I rake my fingers through my hair over and over again, admiring the small mark of rebellion present in my hair.

"I do."

~ (~

"What the hell is that?" Eric questions, tiredness clear in his voice. It's been about a week since the panic-attack-slash-date we had, and I've been pretty much avoiding him since, for the sake of my sanity and my embarrassment.

It's not every day your brother's best friend saves you from a panic attack and takes you on a date. In fact, it pretty much never happens.

"What is what?" I question, walking just a little bit faster through the campus. I was on my way back to the dorm when he caught up with me, so I really have no excuse not to talk to him.

"Your hair."

"It's purple."

"I know that, I mean what did you do to it?" He says, clearly exasperated with me. I self consciously run a hand through the slightly knotted mess of purple, though he grabs my hand away from it immediately and lowers it back down to my side, letting go as soon as it's down as though it'd burned him. "Don't do that, just answer the question."

"Dee and I dyed it. It's temporary—."

"Good, it looks… good." He states, barely getting the words out before someone is by his side, pulling him away from me. I wish I could say that the sight of her pale blonde hair tied up in a perfect high ponytail didn't send a pang of pain through my heart, but I would be lying.

It seems about right, right? A guy like Eric being with a girl like her? I mean, it makes sense. It sounds like a book I would love to read, and I'm sure it would be, if it weren't him…

No. No, it doesn't work that way, this isn't a book.

But once again, I find myself wishing it could be.

But I let it go. I shake away the thoughts and put the headphones that had been bunched in my hands back in my ears. Letting it go.

~ (~

Do you ever wonder what it would be like to fully and completely fall in love? Like, real, true love. Like what you see in the movies where the actors have more chemistry than you could ever imagine. Like what you read about in the best of romance books.

I wonder all of the time. Today especially, I wonder.

Caleb called me early this morning, questioning me on the status of my relationship with Dad. He said that Dad was meant to call me yesterday, though for some reason, he hadn't.

And all over again, I start to wish that my father had never burrowed his way back into my brother's life, and by extension, mine as well. I wish he'd just kept sending me incorrect birthday cards and left me and my family alone. I thought he'd get the hint when I took Mom's last name— when I mailed him the paperwork for the name change and he sent it back signed and sealed, ready to be sent off.

But that isn't what happened. He went and had dinner with Caleb and Eric the other day, apparently, and they'd come to an agreement on something regarding me. I'd like to think that this thing isn't going to affect me at all, but I know it will.

It always does.

"Did he call yet?" Eric questions, coming up behind me a few days later, voice filled with a barely noticeable apprehension.

"No, of course not. He hasn't called me in months, he never does." I find myself complaining. Eric links an arm with mine, pulling me off to the side of the pathway.

"Your brother wants you to move in with us. Joshua, he agreed to pay the fine for you not living on campus."

"What? No! That's insane!" I say, though Eric only shushes me.

"I know, which is why I told them that it was a stupid idea and that you'd never agree. The compromise was dinner. You, Caleb, Joshua and I, our place. Friday night, can you handle that?"

"Jesus, why can't he just stay the hell out of my life?"

"He's your father, Rora."

"No, he's not. He's my sperm donor, that's all. He *left us*. He left me!" I nearly shout. Eric seems to struggle to find something to say for a moment as a tear slips down my face. He barely seems to notice it, his thumb coming up to wipe it from my cheek absentmindedly.

Finally, he seems to figure it out. "If I could make him leave you alone, I would, Rora. I would toss him on a plane back to New York and you'd never have to see him again, if I could, but I can't. This way, you only have to see him once and Caleb won't have you move into the apartment with us."

"He can't make me move in with him either way." I insist, though Eric only shakes his head.

"You're right, but he can try. So please, honey, just come to dinner. We'll figure it all out, everything will be fine. You know Caleb, he just wants to keep you safe. Especially with him going off to New York in a couple of months."

"Do I have to?"

"You kinda do, yeah. I'll figure out a way to get you outta there a little early, though, don't worry."

8

Aurora

Eric's lips press to mine heavily, as if trying to memorize

the shape of them. His hand glides along my back, tickling my spine with light, thoughtful touches that make me wonder if I'm going insane with how giddy they make me feel.

"Tell me you love me, honey." He whispers against my lips before his own stray down, leaving butterfly kisses across my jaw and down to the crook of my neck.

"I love you. I love you." I repeat over and over again, allowing my words to cloud together into a gasp as he kisses me, suckling on the crook of my neck. I'm sure he's leaving a mark on my neck with his bruising kiss, and if I weren't so caught up in the feel of it, I'd be freaked out about how to cover it up.

"Good. Now tell me how much you wish this were real." He
mutters, *continuing his kisses. He barely takes a break to speak,
his lips moving against my neck even through his slightly-muffled
words.*

"I wish this was real, Eric. So much, jus' wanna hold you." I
murmur *through gasps as he continues to kiss me.*

"Good, my pretty girl, 'love you too."

~ (~

The dream certainly isn't the first of its kind. I used to have
them pretty often throughout the beginning of high school. I had
a bit of a crush on my brother's best friend back then, with his
tight smile and dashing good looks. He was the guy everyone
wanted at the time, and the fact that he was Caleb's friend meant
that I was the one who got to spend time with him.

I went over to his house for Sunday brunch. *I* sat with them
at lunch every pizza Friday. *I* was the one he gave rides to school
most mornings.

I had every chance with him, and I knew it. Every chance,
except there was always one thing that prevented my crush on
him from progressing, and that was my brother. He was always
with him, it was the two of them against the world.

But I suppose it's not all bad. Even if I had to get over my
crush on Eric, I could still always talk to him. And now look at
me, on my way to a family dinner with him, Caleb and my dad.

My dad.

I have the sudden urge to call Eric, to try to figure out an excuse not to go to this stupid dinner, though I don't let myself pull out my phone. My brother doesn't ask me for much these days. I've been in college for a month now and I think it's the least we've ever spoken, despite being the closest we've been in two years. He calls about once a week these days, just to ask how I'm doing and if my classes are going okay, then he goes off with his friends from his statistics class.

I barely see him anymore, and I certainly don't hear from him unless it's to talk about my dad or my classes.

I see Eric much more often, though. He's even been coming to sit with me during lunch a couple of days a week, now that he knows that I eat outside instead of in the dining hall.

Finally, Dee pulls up in front of the apartment my brother has made his own over the past month, letting me out on the sidewalk in front of the gigantic apartment building.

If it weren't for my father's money, Caleb and Eric would have never ever been able to afford a place like this, or even anything close to it.

Making my way through the lobby of the slightly over-expensive apartment. It's not often that I let myself dislike something like this. Something that I'm sure is actually absolutely amazing for my brother's life. I love him more than anything, I really, truly do, though the idea of him spending so much time with my father is absolutely terrible.

Speak of the devil and he shall appear, and thankfully, it seems that he's accompanied by his cell phone.

I'm more than happy when he only waves and gives me a wink on our way up in the elevator. Sadly, he gets off the phone within seconds of the door opening.

He walks by my side as I count the doors, finding 137F down several halls and knocking on the door. He doesn't say very much to me as we wait, outside of a polite 'hello, Aurora'.

Thankfully, Eric swings the door open, catching me off guard with his slightly-too-tight charcoal dress shirt and similarly fitted dress pants. I can barely hear Caleb in the background, probably cooking for us. He's a crazy-good cook, always has been.

"Dad, Rory, come in!" Caleb shouts from the other room. Eric hops out of the way as my dad walks into the room, taking a seat on the couch as though he's been here a million times before– which he may or may not have, leaving me to look around the room and examine the apartment my brother lives in. I haven't really been here before, outside of the one time I came over and saw the living room.

The kitchen itself is beautiful, with its lovely modern light fixtures and pale tiles. Caleb stands in front of the stove, a 'kiss the chef' apron tied around his waist and his hands filled with a rather outrageous number of cooking utensils.

Eric's hand flits over the small of my back as I walk past, a comforting gesture. I wish more than anything that I could grab hold of his hand, just to feel the way his skin would feel on mine, comforting me. I want him to hold me again, like he did that night I had the panic attack.

But for now, the feeling of his hand on my back is enough to get me through it.

"So… tell me about school, honey." My father states, his head tilting slightly to the side as he looks at me.

"Don't call me that." I insist without really thinking about it, watching realization and, in some form, sadness, dawn on my father's face.

"Fine, *Aurora*, tell me how school is going."

"It's going fine. I'm enjoying my classes, I've got some pretty nice professors and I've made a couple of friends. My roommate is really awesome, she and I are pretty close." I explain. Eric sends me a kind smile as he watches me fight back the excitement of getting to talk to someone about this. Sure, Caleb asks about classes, but Eric is the only one who ever asks about how I'm doing outside of school. He's had a couple of dinners with Dee and I over the last month and he's the one who seems to be bent on making sure I'm doing alright, despite my brother's promises.

Since that night three weeks ago, Eric has been there for me, which I suppose is both a good and a bad thing. It does nothing for the slowly growing crush I've been developing on him, though it's also becoming the pinnacle of my weeks. It's like I can't help but be excited to talk to him.

"That's really good, hon— Aurora. Eric, how's your photography going, son?"

And thankfully, that takes the attention off of me for a good ten minutes, which I truly wish could last a lifetime. Eric chats idly with my father for a while, Caleb occasionally butting in from the other room where he continues to cook us dinner. Eric tells us all about his photography class and his upcoming projects.

He also sits beside me on one of the two couches in the large room, his knee bumping against mine every couple seconds as if to tell me that he's still here.

My father doesn't seem to notice the growing calm that descends over me like a cloud while I listen to Eric talk, relishing the feeling of his knee bumping against mine in its rhythmic manner.

"Dinner time!" Caleb shouts from the other room after a few minutes, his voice cutting off one of Eric's stories, catching the both of us off guard slightly. Standing up, Eric offers me a hand up from the couch– I don't need it, but it's comforting to feel his hand on mine, even for a short second –and leads the way towards the kitchen fairly slowly. Once my father is a good enough distance away from us, he moves to whisper in my ear, his hot breath tickling the skin of my neck.

"How're you doing, princess? Are you alright?" He asks me quietly, one hand rubbing over my shoulder comfortingly.

No. "Yeah, I'm alright. 'Just wanna get this over with."

"Just say the word and we'll make something up and get you outta here."

~ (~

"Are you sure you want to keep living in the dorm, Aurora? Caleb tells me it's absolutely tiny, and I really am happy to pay–."

"No, really, I like the dorm." I tell him for what feels like the millionth time throughout this dinner. I've tried to keep the attention off of me nearly the entire time, though it hasn't really worked as my father chatters on and on at me. Not really *to* me or *with* me, at me.

Eric sits beside me, watching me diligently as I slowly but surely become frustrated with the task of getting my father off of my back. The man hasn't been in my life for years. I haven't gotten more than one phone call from him and a couple of incorrect birthday cards over the years.

It's like he doesn't realize he isn't my father anymore, he's my sperm donor. He wasn't there for me, all my life, and now he's here to try and upturn the sort-of-life I've built here.

Without thinking, I reach over under the table to lace my fingers with Eric's, taking them from where they rested on his knee and pulling them into my lap. He doesn't so much as move or flinch, not even looking over at me as he continues to say something to Caleb. I wouldn't be his sister if I didn't notice the look my brother gives his best friend as he serves him a second serving of green beans— that same loving look my mother always gave to my father before he left. If it were any other time, I'd feel bad for holding him like this in front of my brother, but I can't seem to care at the moment.

Eric squeezes my hand gently.

"Well, I think I should go ahead and take Aurora home, it's getting kind of late." He says after a moment of thought, interrupting something my dad was saying to Caleb about the Dow Jones stock going down. Neither seem to care much about our hurried exit, giving a wave for us to go.

As soon as we're outside, he pulls me into a tight hug, sort of catching me off guard. Eric's chin rests on the top of my head, my face tucked into his neck and my arms wrapped tightly around his waist. "I'm sorry, princess. I know that sucked."

After a few moments of bliss, we go down to the parking deck, him opening the passenger side door of his car for me before making his way around the 1994 Chevy Impala that he values more than just about anything else and jumping into the driver's seat. As soon as he's turned on the car and gotten out of the space, he tangles his fingers with mine, holding my hand tightly in my lap. One hand on the steering wheel, the other holding me. It's the most romantic feeling in the world, I'm sure, though I doubt he sees it the same way I do. I can't help but stare at the tattoo on his arm. The swirls of ink and the clouds they form— it's just so beautiful, it's hard to handle. For a moment I question why he got it, but I don't have the courage to ask him. Instead, I blurt out a far more awkward question.

"Will you stay with me? Just for a little while? Dee went home for the weekend and I really don't want to be alone right now." I explain hurriedly once he pulls up in front of the dorm.

"I'm not sure that's such a good idea, princess." He says, sighing and tightening his hold on my hand, glancing over at me with a tight frown.

"Please, Eric… I don't want to be alone, not after tonight."

"Just for a little while, alright? I don't want Caleb getting suspicious."

I don't say what I think when he says this, that I want there to be a reason for him to be suspicious. That I want to latch onto him and never let go, that I just want him to hold me and tell me that everything is going to be alright, even though I know it isn't.

Not with Caleb leaving for two months and my father trying desperately to control my life.

"Okay."

And so he holds my hand while he walks me down the hall, pushing the door to my dorm open and pulling me towards the living area.

9

Eric

*G*od, she's the prettiest fucking thing in the world, that's for

certain.

I can't help but stare as she plops her phone into the port, her Spotify playlist popping up on the screen and some song blasting through the speakers. She turns down the music ever so slightly before sitting beside me on the couch, her head dropping onto my shoulder in what seems like exhaustion. I wrap my arm around her shoulders, holding her as close as I can without dragging her onto my lap, allowing myself to breathe in her scent, that same it's been for years. Apples and peppermint, a mixture that's just so uniquely *her.*

"Eric?" She mutters against my skin, and I can't help but shiver at the feeling of her lips brushing lightly against the skin of my neck. Her nose is buried in the crook of my neck, and the feeling of her breath against my skin is more than enough to have me wishing I could hold her without any fear whatsoever, but knowing whose sister she is means I can't.

"Yes, sweetheart?"

"Nothin', never mind." She says after a couple of seconds, clearly having thought better of what she was going to say, though the need to hear what she wants is enough to have me squeezing her shoulders gently, trying to urge it out of her.

"Tell me, sweetheart. I 'wanna hear it."

"If I weren't Caleb's sister would you still like me? I mean, not *like* like, but… would you still spend time with me?" She sputters, clearly a bit embarrassed, and I'm more than thankful that she can't see the warming of my cheeks at her question.

"Yes. If you weren't Caleb's sister, I think I would still spend time with you. Probably more than I do now."

"I'm sorry if I make things awkward with him." She mutters. I can't help myself as I grip her jaw, pulling her up to look me in the eyes.

"No. Don't do that, don't apologize for things that aren't your fault." I tell her, her eyes beaming into mine. I can't help the desire to kiss her pretty lips, just to get a taste, one little taste.

My eyes flit down to her lips and her forehead leans against mine, her eyes slipping shut.

"Would you kiss me if I weren't his sister?" She asks breathily, her voice nothing but a whisper.

"Fuck, princess, ya can't do this to me."

"'Wish you would kiss me."

Just once. Just once. I tell myself as I lean forward just a bit, connecting my lips with hers. She gasps softly at the feeling, letting me explore her lips with my own. Her hand reaches up to tangle in my hair, holding me as close as she can, keeping me entangled in the bruising kiss.

I want to explore her mouth, but I don't let myself. I can't let myself.

So I pull away, watching as she chases the kiss ever so slightly, trying to follow my lips. She pauses before they touch again, pulling away fully and removing her hand from my hair. Her eyes slip open drowsily, her thoughts blindingly clear on her beautiful face.

"I'm sorry, Rora, I shouldn't have done that." I tell her, pulling away a bit further, trying to separate myself from the urge to kiss her again. She does the same, going back to resting her head lightly on my shoulder. It doesn't do much to keep me from wanting to hold her, but at least I can't see her lips anymore.

Fuck, her lips are just perfect.

"I know. I'm sorry."

~ ☾ ~

Fuck. I'm such a fucking idiot.

I wake up in the apartment, not really remembering leaving her dorm or driving back to where I live with my best friend. Her fucking *brother.*

I kissed my best friend's little sister. Fuck, I'm so dead.

And even worse is the fact that I don't regret it, not in the slightest. I can't regret it, not when I once again dreamt about holding her, touching her, kissing her. Certainly not when I remember her chasing my lips with hers, not when I can remember her little gasps like they're completely and utterly ingrained in my memory.

I can hear Caleb whistling in the kitchen, no doubt making us breakfast the way he does every Saturday morning. I'm not sure how to face him today, not when I woke up thinking about his little sister.

"Dude, get your ass up! We've got shit to do!" Caleb shouts through my door after a little while. It's something I'd hoped he wouldn't do, though I knew it would happen. Saturday is Caleb's 'fun day'. He always drags me to some stupid party or bar, and he always ends up needing a ride home afterward.

So I follow his instructions, pulling on a t-shirt and pajama pants and making my way out to where he, my best friend, stands with a plate full of pancakes.

I nearly choke on my pancake when he speaks up a few minutes later. "How was Rora last night? She seemed upset about having to have dinner with Dad."

"She was fine, just a bit anxious, I think."

"Well she must have been somewhat upset. You didn't come back until, like, midnight."

Once again, I nearly fucking choke. I thought he'd been asleep when I came back!

"Jesus, Eric, what the fuck is up with you? Try not to choke!" He says, feigning annoyance and slapping me on the back a couple of times. "I'm glad you stayed with her for a bit, she seems to be getting along with you better now."

"Yeah, well, I've been around." I say, trying desperately to hide the apprehension in my tone.

"I'm glad."

Standing in the large house, I can't help but wish I were anywhere but here. The room is jam packed with people, everyone dancing or shouting just to keep up with their conversations, a spattering of red solo-cups making it clear what sort of event Caleb has managed to drag me into this time.

Speaking of, the man himself disappeared pretty much immediately upon our arrival here, leaving me to mingle with people I don't really know at all.

I recognize a couple of people, though not nearly enough to make me feel comfortable. The floor is sticky with beer and the pressure of bodies all around me is more than enough to make me feel claustrophobic.

I hate things like this. Once again, I allow myself to wish I were with *her*, in her tiny dorm room sitting in her bed or on the couch, just holding her. Maybe we could go back to the park, I'd much prefer that to where I am right now.

The music is loud and booming, vibrating the floor beneath me. It's the exact opposite of what I listened to last night, when I was with her. It's loud and annoying and horrifically techno-based.

I wish I was anywhere but here.

But mostly, I wish I was with *her*.

Grabbing a solo cup and filling it with some form of off-brand Dr. Pepper, —Prof. Salt, because that's super creative— I make my way out onto the back porch, finding a smattering of couples gathered around in one corner playing some stupid card game and a couple of groups scattered around the lawn in various states, ranging from conversation to straight-up wrestling.

There's a bench against one of the railings that isn't home to anyone at the moment, so that's where I end up, sitting down and shoving a shirt out of my way, sipping on my soda and trying to ignore my blossoming headache.

My phone buzzes in my pocket, and I almost ignore it, before realizing that a girl across the porch had fully removed her shirt and bra, so I decide to distract myself from that issue with whatever notification I just received.

And low and behold, it's from *her.*

Aurora: What are you doing right now?

Eric: I'm at a party with Caleb, why?

Aurora: Come over.

Eric: I can't, princess.

Eric: Caleb will kill me.

Aurora: I don't care what he says, I just want to be with
     you.

I want to let myself believe, if only for a moment, that she means *really* be with me, though I know that's not the case.

Eric: What happened?

Aurora: Gray came over to talk to me. Can you please
     come get me?

Fuck.

Fuck. Fuck. Fuck. Fuck. Fuck.

So I do. I search for Caleb first, obviously, and he tells me that he can stay here with one of his friends (after hearing that I have a last-minute project to finish, not that I'm going to go see his sister at 11 o'clock at night), so I leave. My knuckles are white as I hold onto the wheel, driving across town to her building, rushing through the halls towards her dorm.

Everything looks to be fine from the outside, though as soon as she opens the door, I can see the tears rushing down her beautiful face. Before I can so much as reach for her, she's launched herself into my arms, nearly knocking me over as she presses her lips to mine roughly.

"What did he say?" I break away to ask her, though she just brings me back into the bruising kiss, her hands tingling in my hair and pulling slightly at the roots, bringing a small groan from my lips. Grabbing her hips, I force myself to pull her away from me a bit, watching as she tries to hide her pinkening cheeks from me.

"That he didn't mean to stand me up, that he's sorry, that he had something to do. I probably would have believed him, too, but he told me he saw us driving around together last night and that's why he came over." She tells me as I brush my thumb over her soft cheeks, wiping away her tears.

"I'm sorry, princess." I tell her, pulling her into the dorm. She follows me without thought, though when I try to go to the small living area, she pulls me into her room instead. It's a truly tiny space, probably only 10 x 10 feet overall, but she seems to have made it her own. She's added a couple of things since I was last here, including a bunch of tacked-up photos, more than one of them including me.

She kisses me again, pulling me away from my examination of the room and into her arms.

It's not going to be just once.

She calms down after a while, just letting me hold her tightly as we lean against the wall beside her bed, propped up on pillows with our feet hanging off the edge. Well, her feet and about half of each of my calves, since I'm a good foot taller than her.

"I really like kissing you." She tells me quietly, leaning over to peck my lips.

"I know, honey, I really like kissing you too, but we can't. You know we can't."

"Why not? Why can't we just be together? I've had a crush on you basically all my life, why can't we just be happy together?"

"You know why, sweetheart." I tell her, trying to ignore the blooming heat in my chest at the thought of her pining over me in our childhood.

I always had a bit of a thing for her too.

"Do I? 'Cause I think Caleb can fuck off."

"He can't though, Aurora. We can't do this to him." I tell her gently, though everything in me wants to go back to kissing her.

I leave shortly after that, hating the fact that I can't stay with her. Something in me wants to, like really wants to. Like we're two magnets that can't help but be pulled together.

10

Aurora

$\mathcal{E}$ric's eyes fill with something along the lines of joy as we drive, his hand finding its home in my own as we make our way towards the mall, a place called Southpoint. Caleb's birthday is in a couple of days, and since it's been a while since I got to celebrate with him, I decided I had to get him the best birthday present possible.

Eric– after some begging on my part –agreed to join me on my shopping spree.

Since last weekend, I've been seeing more and more of him. He eats lunch with me most days, he comes over to my dorm to study, and we share more and more secretive kisses that make me wish over and over again for something more.

Still, the fear that Caleb will find out and be mad, or worse, *murderous,* hasn't left us. Eric still treats me like his best friend's sister most of the time, and despite all of it, I want more and more of him. I want to hold him and kiss him and fall asleep in his arms, but I can't. I know I can't.

But more than that, I want him to want to be with me.

It isn't particularly fair to wish for this, I know that. I know that he doesn't want to —that he *can't* betray my brother's trust — but that doesn't make me want him any less. His pale blue eyes fuel dreams most nights, his words making me think for hours, often about the most idiotic things like his idea of genetically modifying carnivorous plants to fix overpopulation. Sometimes it's his hands that distract me, or his lips– actually, it's his lips pretty damn often.

Sometimes it's everything about him.

As we pull up in front of the mall, I can't help but laugh as he has to re-park once or twice after barely getting into a spot. We're even honked at once, and he gives up after a couple of minutes, not bothering to change the way his Impala sits lopsided in a space.

He doesn't stop himself from holding my hand as we walk towards the towering buildings ahead of us, and I don't want to stop him. His fingers twist together with mine, making butterflies flutter around in my stomach, quite possibly having brawls with the way it makes the anxiety spike and my throat tighten.

"So, where're we headed, princess?"

~ ⟨ ~

Kohls, the Gap, Urban Outfitters, and a small candy shop later, we've each managed to find Caleb a gift, though Eric's smile has dropped with every tiny gift he's purchased for his best friend.

"Does this say 'sorry for kissing your sister' to you?" he asks jokingly, holding up a dark brown wallet with several slots for credit cards for me to look at.

"Nope." I say, popping the P as I grab another wallet off the rack in front of us, one covered in little pink flowers. "But this one does."

He chuckles lightly, laying a kiss to my forehead before we leave the shop. It's the first one we haven't found anything substantial at, and I can tell we're both feeling just a little bit dejected and tired.

Finally, we make it to the last store on our list, a small shop which seems to be filled with everything from adult *stuff* to graphic t-shirts, which Eric was insistent that we go to. He immediately walks to the back of the store, telling me to look at the t-shirts for a minute while he picks something up.

The wall is covered in t-shirt designs, most on the more explicit side, though a few of them are just funny. Several are covered in periodic table jokes– a few of them spelling out curse words –and there are a lot that just make bad puns.

Beside the t-shirt rack, though, is something that catches my eye. There's a shelf covered in different lighters, some made in fun shapes and others simply with designs or pictures.

There are probably hundreds of them just on this wall alone. One has the playboy bunny, another, a marijuana leaf. One has a picture of a girl on a motorcycle and the one beside it just says 'badger'. On the bottom of the shelf is one with a bunch of vines etched into the side. It's a flip-top one, and it reminds me, oddly, of the matches my English professor gave me so long ago. They still sit untouched in my things, though I think of them more often than I probably should. They're just matches, really; they shouldn't mean too much to me. The bottom of the lighter is inscribed with a short saying, and it makes my throat tighten in the way it reminds me of what she had told me. *Even old souls have to pretend to be young at some point.*

Perhaps it isn't too much to say that I haven't kept up the feeling I had that night. The feeling of pure adrenaline rushing through my veins at having done something I knew I wasn't supposed to do. The feeling of excitement and regret and happiness. No one had ever called me an old soul before her, but now I can't seem to stop thinking about it. Not with a small matchstick doodled on every paper I get handed back.

"You're not going to steal that are ya, peach?" A gruff voice startles me, though I turn to see a rather put-together man. He seems to be around my age, his pale-brown hair swept back and gelled to perfection, his polo top tucked into his khakis.

"Of course not."

"Good, I'm glad. Wouldn't want you sullying your good name. Can I help you find anything?"

"Do you work here?" I ask, glancing over his chest in search of a name tag, though there isn't one.

"Nope, my parents own the place. Now, can I help you find anything, peach?" He repeats himself.

"I'm looking for a gift for my brother. It's his birthday in a couple days and it's the first time in years I get to celebrate it with him, you know?"

"I do." He says abruptly, turning and walking towards the back of the store. He doesn't even look over his shoulder to make sure I'm following him as I scurry after him. He leads me right up to the back wall and over to a small display of frames, each one more extravagant looking than the last. Some are made up of gold or clay shaped into marijuana leaves, some are covered in curse words or flames.

There's one at the bottom of the stack, though, that catches my eye. It's covered in pale blue and pink shells, faux pearls sprinkled in in some places.

That's the one I grab.

"Not what I was expecting, but you do you I guess. What's your name, peach?"

"Aurora!" And with that, Eric is at my side. "I thought you were looking at t-shirts, princess." He says, glancing over me before turning to the man in front of me. "Who the fuck are you?"

"Eric!"

"Chill, man, just helpin' her out, not trying to take her from you. I'm Jase, by the way, peach– er, Aurora." The man— Jase —says, reaching forward to shake my hand, then Eric.

"We're going, Rora. I got what I needed." He says in a rough voice, his hand finding my elbow in an attempt to shoo me towards the doors, though I hold my footing.

"I'm not ready to go yet! I'm thinking about getting this frame, what'a ya think?"

"It's a bunch of shells, Rora. Do you really need to spend twenty bucks on a frame covered in shells?" He asks, swiping an angry hand through his wavy blonde hair.

"I thought he might like it. I was gonna put that photo you took of me on Wednesday in it." I try to explain, though he cuts me off.

"No, Aurora. Caleb can't know about that, you know that. Now let's go."

"Why can't he know you eat lunch with me?"

"I walked into more drama than I was expecting with you, peach." Jase says, though he goes ignored by me. Eric sends him a glare.

"Fuck off, man. He just can't know, Rora, so can we please just go?"

I can almost see the jealousy and anger raging behind his eyes.

"No. You go ahead, I'll catch the bus back to campus when I'm done."

He blanks at this, looking down at me in obvious confusion. "Aurora, you know why he can't know, can we please just leave? I'll buy you all the shell frames in the fucking world, can we just get out of here? This guy is pissing me off."

"Dude, she said no." Jase says, receiving another piercing glare from Eric.

"Back the hell off, fuckface."

"What are you, a fucking idiot? She said *no*, numskull, leave 'er alone!" Jase insists, though I try to step between them immediately, trying to avoid the fight I know can occur when Eric gets angry like this.

"Do you not wanna leave with me, honey?" Eric asks me numbly, continuing to glare over my shoulder at Jase.

"I'm sorry, of course. Of course." I murmur, handing Jase the frame and trying to walk away, though he grabs my arm immediately.

"Not a chance. You, dude, need to leave before I call the fucking cops. Get your shit straight, she said she doesn't want to leave with you, so go. You're not her fucking dad, you can't go around treating her like this."

Eric ends up leaving me behind in the small store, tears trickling down my face as I watch him leave. Jase stands behind me, watching as I fiddle with the shell frame, trying to figure out what to do from here. I didn't think this through very well. The buses don't run this late on Sundays, and I can't call Caleb, he'll know Eric left me behind here.

Once I've purchased the shell frame– and spent ten minutes crying in the back-room of the store, I make my way back towards where I know Eric parked, hoping to find a cab or something, though I've got no such luck. It's already getting dark out, and the sight of the gleaming Impala in one of many empty spaces sends a shiver down my spine.

Eric sits leaning against his car, watching me walk closer and closer. As soon as I'm close enough, he stands up, pulling me into a tight hug.

"I'm sorry, honey. I shouldn't have yelled at you."

Everything in me screams to tell him it's okay, but I know it isn't.

I need an explanation.

"It's fine, can we just go?"

So he drives me home in silence, his hands kept securely on his side of the car, never once straying to touch my own. He parks in a spot in front of the dorm, both of us staying put in our seats despite the tension.

"Why did you do it?"

"I was jealous." He tells me simply, not bothering to look at me. "You were supposed to be with the t-shirts and you weren't, then I turn around and you're with some *guy*, and he's calling you *peach*."

"He was just helping me pick something out for Caleb."

"No, Rora, he was flirting with you." Eric explains with a sigh.

"Even if he was, why would it matter? You've made it pretty clear, Eric, I'm not a risk you're willing to take."

"*Fuck*, princess, do you think I don't know that? You think I don't know that he could fucking touch you and kiss you all he wanted if you let him, while every time I hold your hand I have to feel guilty about it? It's terrible, sweetheart. I dream about you and I wake up hating myself, I kiss you and I feel like I'm hurting my best friend. It's the worst, and I can't help but keep doing it because you're all I ever think about!" He says, clearly trying to restrain himself as his anger begins to really show, alongside his despair.

"What, you think I don't feel it too?" I nearly shout at him. "You think I don't notice when that blonde girl goes around touching your arm? You think I don't want to touch you every single time I see you? This is painful, Eric, because we'd be so good together, and the only thing holding us back is the one person who wants both of us to be happy."

"Just not with each other."

11

Aurora

*W*ith Thanksgiving around the corner, my fear of going

home has only grown. It's been hard, with my mom barely

calling me and Eric avoiding me— not to mention the fact that

Caleb has decided to go visit our dad for the holiday instead of

coming home.

Thanksgiving break starts in exactly two days, which means

a three and a half hour car ride home with Eric (Caleb

volunteered him to drive me home, since we live next door), and

then a week at home, with my mother. *Only* my mother.

Pulling my hat down over my head and grabbing the cherry

chapstick that's made a home in my pocket with the cold

weather, I prepare myself for the cold I'm about to face outside of the English hall. Lit 101 took a bit less time than usual, and there aren't many people outside, which makes my walk back to the dorm both better and worse.

It's the last day of classes for the week, or, mine, at least, and I left all of the packing for the holiday to do today, so that's what I'm prepared for when I make it back to the dorm room.

Not to find Eric sitting on the couch in my living room, chatting with Dee thoughtfully. How she got back here before me, I've got no clue, since we're in the same class, though that's barely even on my mind as their conversation stalls.

"Hey, I just came over to remind you, we need to leave pretty early on Sunday. I wanna beat the traffic as much as we can." He tells me cooly, as though he hasn't been avoiding me as much as he can over the past month.

He still calls and texts me, gives me rides, and eats lunch with me, though he's been more distant than he used to be. We share occasional forbidden kisses when one of us needs the comfort, but it's like he's there but he's not, at the same time.

I miss when he was here, fully. I miss when his kisses were filled with warm passion, not this fearful, cold need whenever he's upset about something.

But having him at all is better than nothing.

"I have a cell phone, Eric." I tell him, flinching as Dee groans loudly.

"I know that, princess."

"Would you two quit messing around and just talk about it already? Spending time with you is like walking on broken glass, get over it! Either tell Caleb you're into each other or get over it."

"He'll kill me." Eric says simply. "He'll kill me; he loves her, more than anything."

"As if you don't give two shits about her? Jesus, you're an idiot, man. Caleb is not the one stopping you two from being together, you are."

~ (~

Dee has a point, that's for sure. As Eric pulls the car up in front of the dorm building and helps me get my overly-packed suitcase into the trunk, I can't help but think about just how much of a point she has. She's right, and I kind of hate it. Just a little bit.

Caleb is about to leave for a while. The question is whether or not I'm gonna be able to let him go again after that time.

He doesn't reach over and take my hand as we pull out of the parking lot the way he did when we went to the mall. He barely says a word to me other than asking if I want coffee.

After a quick stop at the Starbucks, we're on our way, both dreading the three hour car ride back home. Eric puts on some music, Nirvana playing softly through the speakers as we get onto the freeway.

"I thought you hated Nirvana."

He grunts, shaking his head as he switches lanes expertly, getting around a rather slow truck. "No, that's Caleb. I love 'em."

"Oh."

He takes a deep breath, seeming to think over something before speaking up again, his voice slightly shaking as he talks. "Give me two months, sweetheart."

"What?"

"Two months. Caleb leaves in two weeks, give me those two months. We'll go out, we won't have to be afraid of him figuring it out. We'll see what it's like."

"You want to go out with me?"

"Of course. In two weeks. I'll drive your brother to RDU and I'll come get you, we'll go out." He says stiffly, as if trying to hold something back.

"What about this week? Caleb isn't here now."

He thinks it over for a moment, placing his hand gently on my knee. "We'll play it by ear. We'll be careful, but I don't think I can stay away from you. Not if he isn't around to make me feel guilty. We both know your mom isn't gonna give a shit either way— if she even notices."

The sick truth of the statement makes my stomach hurt, but I only nod. He seems to realize the pain that statement inflicts, as he reaches over immediately and rubs a thumb over mine, tangling our fingers together.

~ (~

The house looks the exact same as I remember it, though without my mother. She left a note on the door telling me she'd gone to the grocery store and to let myself in, so I'm not surprised to find all of the lights off and the house completely empty.

She hasn't added so much as a throw pillow in the last two months.

"This is sort of… eerie." Eric says, hauling my suitcase into the house. I told him I'd get it, but he was insistent, so I settle for carrying my bag of laundry.

"Eric?"

"Yes, sweetheart?" He asks, setting the trunk down in the foyer.

"We're alone. Kiss me."

And he does, gently at first, though it progresses into something rough and needy as he holds tightly to my waist, swallowing my sounds as I do his. My fingers tangle in his hair, and his hand moves to cup the back of my neck, holding me as close as he can to himself.

Slowly, his lips slip from mine and move down my jaw, then my neck.

"You're gonna be the death of me, honey." He murmurs against my neck, teeth scraping against my flesh lightly. "I'm gonna have to get on medicaid."

"'M sorry."

"I'm not." He says simply. "I wanna take you out tomorrow, we can walk around downtown. We'll go to the pier or something. We could go to that restaurant you like too, Provision, right?"

"Okay." I find myself muttering quietly, pulling him back to my lips.

"You know I'm falling for you, right?"

$\sim$ ⟨ $\sim$

As it turns out, it isn't just the house that's the same as when I left. Mom is the exact same woman she was two months ago as she walks into the living room carrying bags of groceries. Eric stands up from his place on the couch immediately, pausing the movie we were watching and going to grab some of the many groceries from her.

"Aurora, good, you're here." My mom says simply, putting a very large turkey in the fridge. "Tell me about your classes."

"Hey, Mom. They're going pretty good."

"How is archaeology?"

"It's good. I'm taking natural biology right now, though, not archaeology."

"Good. And how's your personal life? Staying focused on school?"

"I've been sort of seeing this guy, but that's it. And Dee and I are doing well, we've gotten really close." I relay to her, regretting the first part as soon as she questions me on his name.

"Who is he? Is he going to come down for Thanksgiving? We already have the Meridians over but I can certainly set another seat."

"No, no, that's not necessary. He isn't coming."

~ (~

"You look perfect, sweetheart." He tells me for what feels like the millionth time as I show off yet another dress, looking for the perfect one to wear for Thanksgiving dinner.

Eric lays on my twin-sized mattress, the pale pink duvet squished under him as he rests on the bed, his hands linked together behind his head and his legs crossed.

We went down to the boardwalk this morning to look for dresses in some of the fancy boutiques that have overrun the old fishing town, though I couldn't find a single one I liked, so we ended up back at the house looking through my closet.

Well, I'm looking through my closet. He's resting.

"What about that red one you wore to the playground?" He questions, watching me toss another dress aside.

"My mother would have my head if I wore that, Eric. It's not exactly Thanksgiving appropriate."

"I think it's hot."

"Yeah, well, my mom would not."

"Fine, then wear the blue one. Right there." He says, pointing out one of the few dresses I haven't tried on for him yet. He receives a sigh in return as I climb into the bed beside him, ignoring the pain in my joints as I rest my head on his chest.

"I like this." I tell him quietly, expecting him to scoff or chuckle at me, though he only nods, wrapping his arm around me and laying a chaste kiss to the top of my head.

"I do too, princess. I do too."

"Why do you always call me that? Is it because of my name? Because I was named for the northern lights, not the princess." I find myself saying, questioning him.

"No, I know that, princess. It's because you're like a sweet little princess. You just run around being happy and innocent and no one can tell you that the world sucks, because you just can't see it."

"I can't see it?"

"No, sweetheart, you really can't. You're just such a sweet girl– that was a bad choice of words."

"What, because I'm a girl I can't be tough? I can't see what's going on in the world?" I question, trying to force an edge into my tone, though he doesn't even seem to notice it.

"That's not—."

"I'll have you know, I'm a lot stronger than you seem to think. I'm not some helpless girl who can't do a thing on her own! I've seen shitty things happen, asshat."

"Aurora, I didn't say that! It's just, you've always been so–."

"So what, Eric? Spit it out!" I nearly shout at him, having sat up on the bed while I stare down at him, making my anger clear.

"You know what I mean, you're just so– kind."

"Or blind, you mean? How could you say something like that? That I don't see the bad things in the world? What do you think it was like for me to lose my father? He up and left me, Eric, did you just forget about that?"

"It's not a shameful thing, Aurora, you just need a lot of looking after sometimes. You're *naive*." He defends idiotically.

"What the hell is wrong with you? Get out of my house, now!"

"Aurora–."

"Now, Eric. Take that for whatever you want to, but I'm telling you to get the *hell* out of my house. Right now." I say, walking into the bathroom and locking myself inside, just to get away from him.

I always knew I came off as weak to a lot of people. My brother has always been around to take care of me, to make sure I've been alright. Sometimes I forget that Eric was there too, that he was with my brother all along and that he has always believed that my brother was the only thing that ever kept me from getting injured or killed or whatever.

I can hear him fumbling around in my bedroom for a good few minutes before the sound of the door opening and closing takes over, feeling almost deafening to my injured mind.

Happiness isn't naivete. It never has been and it never will be. My happiness does not make me naive to the world around me. I know what's happening, I know what's going on.

Screw him.

~ ☾ ~

Sitting across from Eric that night at Thanksgiving dinner is pure hell, for the both of us, I'm sure.

He keeps looking up at me awkwardly, as if he's trying to say something with his beautiful blue eyes, though I won't meet them so he can't get it across.

He thinks I'm fucking *naive.*

Honestly, It's not as much that I'm surprised as that I'm pissed off. It isn't like he's been around for the last couple of years, so I'm not sure what he thinks he has the right to judge me on, but it certainly isn't my strength.

I've never spent much time thinking about being strong, though I know I am. I'm more than strong, actually, I'm tough. I've gone through shit he doesn't even know about, how could he think I'm weak? A guy who can't even stand to be around me without feeling guilty for being attracted to me? What the hell is wrong with him?

As if he can read my mind, he glances away, returning his gaze to his mother and little cousin, both of whom sit with us around the large round dining table.

12

Aurora

To say that I'm annoyed would be a massive

understatement. In fact, to say anything at all about it would be an understatement, because I'm so angry I can hardly think.

Naive. He called me naive. Naive.

Okay, so I'll be honest. I've always known that maybe I don't see the world the same way my brother and Eric do. I've known all my life that I see through the eyes of someone looking for beauty in everything, while they look for flaws in the very natural world they live in. I'm sure it's what's always made them worry about me; that I don't pay as much attention to everything wrong with the world, but I have to say…

I don't think there's anything wrong with being an optimist. I think that he's an idiot for thinking I'm *naive* just because I don't see things the same way he does.

I see things that are wrong, I really do. I see the way people look at me like I'm a complete and utter moron sometimes and I know that I'm a clutz and I don't work well with others and I'm a huge jerk sometimes. I don't do the best job of standing up for myself, so much so that Gemma always used to call me a doormat, though that was back when she could bother to pick up the phone. Now all I ever see of her is her Instagram account, which usually just consists of pictures of her and her new friends on the beach, often wearing very small swimsuits the size of postage stamps.

I know what's wrong with the world. I really do.

Eric sits beside me in silence as we make the three hour journey back to campus, him keeping his hands on the steering wheel the entire time, never venturing to hold my hand or lay his heavy palm on my knee. He keeps quiet nearly the whole time, listening to his Nirvana CD a good three or four times before we make it back to my dorm room.

He doesn't carry my suitcase this time.

I don't give two shits, since apparently he only does it because he thinks I'm weak.

"You know I didn't mean it like that, right?" He asks me after a moment of silence, walking beside me towards my dorm room, which is far towards the end of the building compared to the door we just came in to. Neither of us mention it, but we both know he parked in the wrong spot and that's why it's taking us so long to get to my dorm.

"Mean it like what, Eric? Like I'm just some incompetent girl you need to take care of? You called me *naive,* for fuck's sake."

"I didn't mean to offend you, it's just— you always—."

"I always what, Eric?" I ask with a grunt, sliding my key into the lock on the dorm. Dropping my suitcase right inside the door, I turn to look at him, finding immediately that he's still standing outside, though I had expected him to come inside.

He doesn't get further than the doorway, his arms coming to cross over his chest as he stares me down. "You've always been his little sister to me! Can you blame me for thinking you're a bit naive, Aurora? You're Caleb's clumsy little sister, that's what I've always known you as. I'm still getting used to you being… this!" He shouts.

"Being what, Eric? Being an adult, having purple hair, what?"

He groans, running a hand through his tousled hair. "Being gorgeous! Being so incredibly attractive that I can't help wanting to jump you every time I fucking see you? Can you blame me,

Aurora? Do you not see yourself? I'm used to taking care of you, not wanting you! I'm turning into the kind of guy Caleb has always wanted me to keep away from you!"

"I don't want you to protect me, I want you to be with me!" I shout right back at him, feeling the burn of hot, wet tears gathering in my eyes. "If I wanted a protector I would be spending time with my brother, I just want *you!*"

He grunts out a laugh at the thought before turning on his heel, though he speaks up one more time before walking away. "You don't want me, Aurora. You want someone, and I'm cutting it for you. That's all. It's only a few more days, I'll drive *your brother* to the airport and then we'll discuss this. But don't you dare fucking lie to me, Aurora. You do *not* want me. You want to feel like you're doing something wrong because it makes you feel like the fucking shit."

"Don't walk away from me! I'm talking to you, Eric!" I shout after him, rushing out the door to catch up with his much longer strides.

He thinks he's so tough.

"Is it too much for me to ask that you just leave me the hell alone, Aurora? All I want is for all of this to just stop for a couple days, and here you are thinking you have any right *whatsoever* to be pissed with me."

I stop immediately, wanting nothing more than to not feel a sense of fault for this, despite the fact that it was him who caused it. "You called me naive!"

"You *are* naive! All you ever do is act naive, Aurora! You think no one notices that you always act like you don't have a care in the world, but we do! You think Gray didn't notice that you act like a *fucking* child?"

"What are you saying, that it's my fault?"

He sighs, running an angry hand through his hair. "That's exactly what I'm saying, Aurora. If you weren't such a *child* you wouldn't need protection! Gray fucked with you because he knows you wouldn't do a fucking thing about it. Caleb knows it too, I know it, your mom knows it."

"Stop it! Stop yelling at me! I *know!*"

"No, you don't!" He shouts. "You don't know because you refuse to see! You are the exact definition of *naive*, Aurora! You see the world like a love story, but it isn't! There's a reason everyone else sees it as hell!"

"I don't think that's my fault!"

"It is, though! It is because you refuse to see it! You think I'm an asshole to call you naive, but I'm not! It's who you are, and I don't hate it, Aurora! I never meant to hurt your feelings, but you and I both know I'm right! You. Are. Naive!"

And with that, I'm done. I want to scream at him, to cry and shout and kick and make a fuss, but I don't. "Fuck you, Eric."

And I leave. I want to look back at her. Hell, I want to run back to her, but I don't. I push my hair out of my eyes and I turn around and I walk away.

~ (~

I'd like to say that the argument last night didn't make me hate myself even more, but I'd be lying if I did. I'm used to feeling this way, sort of, though the feeling isn't made better by that fact.

Eric will be here to pick me up in almost exactly 48 hours, to take me on a *date*.

I'm not even sure if I should open the door for him if he shows up. I'm not even sure if he *will* show up.

Pulling on a pair of jeans and my Nirvana shirt, I pack up a few things and make my way out of the dorms. Thanksgiving break is still on for a few more days, so I'm pretty much alone on campus, outside of a couple of stragglers.

Dee won't be home for four days, but my mom insisted we go on home. She said she needed to focus on the upcoming Thanksgiving banquet that her company throws every year— though somehow, I doubt that that's the complete truth. I think she didn't want me there.

I take an Uber to the mall, not wanting to call anyone with a car. I find the store I met Jase in, immediately walking to the back where I know there is a display of disposable cameras, each going for about thirty bucks. I grab two, taking them to the counter and grabbing a lighter on the way, the one I had looked at a month and a half ago. It's still there, much to my surprise, and its price isn't enough to stop me from buying it. Jase is nowhere in sight as I check out, a blonde girl with thick, intricate eyeliner hands me my things in a cheap plastic bag with the store's logo on it —a turtle saying 'yeah, bruh' with a joint hanging from its mouth. Its eyes are even slightly reddened and puffy, the details being slightly over exaggerated and annoying to look at.

"Have a nice day, come back soon." She tells me, though her heart clearly isn't in it. I leave the store with my bag in hand, not really caring that I probably looked like a weirdo buying two cameras, a lighter and a bag of Reese's-Pieces. Though the woman seemed to be just a little bit high, so I don't think she cared all that much.

Two months. That's what I have to look forward to. 38 more hours, then I'll have two months with Eric.

~ (~

I paint them on the floor of my dorm room, a paper bag cut open and spread out in front of me and a couple of bottles of cheap acrylic sat up on top of it. I squeeze out some of each color on a paper plate from the dining hall, painting flowers and smiley faces and pale blue clouds and peace signs all over both of the cameras, letting them both dry and coating them in some cheap clear varnish before wrapping one of them up with tissue paper, which I grabbed from a Dollar-General on the way home from the mall. The Uber driver was unimpressed with the stop and insisted I pay another five dollars for the trouble, though he took it down to two when I said I'd give him a bad review. I normally wouldn't do such a thing, but Eric's words from last night still stick in my mind, constantly reminding me that he doesn't think I'm strong enough to make my way in the world. To stand up for myself. I may have taken it a tiny little bit too far with the threat, though.

Two months. I've got two months with him. Two months.

32 hours left. I finish up by painting my initials on the bottom edge of the lighter in pale blue, stowing it away with the matches given to me by my English professor so long ago. It was only a few months, technically, but it feels like a long time ago.

~ (~

31 hours. I eat dinner alone, waiting for the day I can have dinner with *him.*

29 hours. I go to sleep, alone, waiting for when I can sleep beside *him.*

19 hours. I wake up alone, waiting for when I can wake up beside *him.*

2 hours. I sit alone on the couch, waiting for him to show up. Caleb's flight leaves in almost exactly four hours, so they'll be on the way to RDU pretty soon.

And then he shows up, knocking on my door and pulling me into a tight hug as soon as it swings open. I wrap my arms around his neck, digging my face into his shoulder and inhaling his soft smell. I love the feeling more than I ever could have imagined, being able to hold him close like this. I love it more than anything.

"I'm sorry, sweetheart. I shouldn't have yelled at you like that." He tells me softly, pulling me up so my legs are wrapped around his waist, his hands moving to hold me up by my thighs.

"It's okay." I say, just happy to have him in my arms. "I have a present for you."

"Yeah? You didn't have to do that, Rora."

"If we're doing this, we're doing it right." I jump down out of his arms, tangling my fingers with his and leading him to the living area, plugging my phone into the music player and listening as my music immediately begins playing quietly. Finally, I grab the gift, placing it in his hands.

He rips into it immediately, smiling as he catches sight of the painted camera. "What's this for, princess?" He asks me, picking it up to examine it. I realize then that he, as a photographer, has several cameras a thousand times better than this one, though that doesn't matter much at the moment.

"Two months, two cameras. We'll take as many photos as we can, and then in two months, we split ways if that's what we decide to do." I say, my voice sounding surprisingly severe. "I want to be able to remember everything if this doesn't work out. I want the memories."

"Okay. Two months, two cameras." He agrees, pulling me down into his lap.

13

Aurora

$\mathcal{D}$ay 1 of dating Eric.

Eric takes me to the diner, with his hair gelled back on the top of his head and his arms on show for me to see the three or four tattoos he has on the left one, one of which is a fork. He tells me that he used to steal them from restaurants when he was little, that it was his vice.

I tell him I want to get one myself. One of a dandelion, on my shoulder. I tell him that I used to really like dandelions as a kid.

He tells me he'll make an appointment with his tattoo artist for me if I want him to.

I tell him about the book I'm working on.

He tells me why he's so interested in photography, why he's studying anthropology (his dad made him). He asks me why I love to write so much.

I tell him the truth. That the fantasy of it is so much better than the reality of the world I live in. I tell him about that night with my English teacher, about feeling alive for the first time in so long. He chastises me for smoking but says he understands— that growing up he was always told he was a bit of an old soul.

He tells me that he and his mom were in an accident when he was five, that her back was messed up now and that she was always complaining about it, but she never regretted it because that night in the hospital, they realized he had pneumonia and really needed antibiotics. He tells me that he's always really careful with driving, and that he never ever picks up his phone while he's on the road.

I tell him that I have a birthmark on my left butt cheek.

He tells me he has one on his lower back that his older brother used to call his 'tramp stamp'. He tells me that now he has a little boy named Brandon, that the kid is basically a squirrel as a human being. He tells me that the little kid really likes water fountains, so his sister-in-law put one in the pool in their backyard and sends him videos of the kid staring at it.

I tell him that Caleb has always hated kids, and it makes me sad sometimes that I won't be able to spoil a little niece or nephew rotten and be the cool auntie.

He tells me that he was at the hospital with his brother for twenty eight hours while his wife was in labor, and that he and his family were exhausted afterward. He tells me that he slept for hours when they got home.

He was sixteen.

I tell him that I really love kids but I'm scared of having one.

He asks if it's because of my mom and dad.

I tell him how my mom always used to tell me that I should stop dreaming big because I'll have further to fall when I don't make it. I tell him that I used to sit up waiting for my dad to tuck me in every night when I was little, only for Caleb to do it. I tell him that I quit waiting when I was twelve years old. I ask him what the cloud tattoo is for and tell him how much I love it.

He tells me that he got it as soon as he turned eighteen, on a dare from his brother. He won't tell me what the dare is, but he does say that he has one more tattoo on his chest. He promises that he'll show it to me sometime.

He tells me that he hated Caleb when he first met him, but that he thought I was, quote on quote, 'pretty cool for a girl.'

He tells me that he thinks I'm pretty cool in general now.

He tells me that I'm a really good kisser, that he really wants to keep kissing me forever.

I tell him that I really really like kissing him too.

And he kisses me.

~ (~

Day 3 of dating Eric.

His lips move down my shoulders, down my left arm, back up to my neck. My arms wind around his neck.

"I love this dress on you, sweetheart." He tells me in between kisses, pulling slightly on the dark purple fabric that falls down to the area just above my knees. His hands sit gingerly on my waist, pulling away from me slightly.

"We have a movie to catch." I tell him quietly, halfway hoping he doesn't hear me, but he does. He leaves one last chaste kiss on my lips before moving me off of his lap– scooching me, really.

"Come on, sweetheart."

I stand up quickly, turning around just in time to catch sight of the camera flash as he takes a quick photo of me. He catches my hair whipping around perfectly. The smiley faces I painted on the front of the camera stare back at me as I lean down to kiss him one more time, his lips following mine slightly as I pull back.

"We have a movie to catch."

~ ☾ ~

Day 6 of dating Eric.

I can't help but panic. I know, I know, it doesn't exactly make sense, but that's how it's turned out.

It's been six days of dating Eric and I already hate the idea of letting go of him, of leaving him. I know it will kill me to release him, to walk away when my brother gets home, though I know it won't work out the way we both want it to. There are too many people involved, too many hearts that could be broken, my brother being the highest on my list.

Maybe the reason I can't help but panic is that I know my brother would hate me if he knew about the man I'm falling for. The man I've been enjoying kissing, the one I'm taking photographs of every single day because selfishly, I never want to forget the way he makes me feel, the way he makes my heart skip a beat.

Caleb would kill me if he ever found out what I'm doing right now. How I'm feeling. He would never forgive me, never trust me again. He's known Eric since we were kids, he's his best friend. I know more than anything just how much this would ruin him.

I don't think I could possibly live with myself if this messed up his friendship with Eric.

So yeah, I'm panicking. I'm panicking really, really bad.

And it doesn't make it any easier knowing that my brother is the one I would normally call in this situation, but I can't. I can't call him because I'm betraying him.

So I do the next best thing. I sit on the floor of my very small bathroom, my only thought being the fact that my best friend, my brother, the guy I grew up with, is going to hate me if he ever finds out what I'm doing.

~ ☾ ~

Day 7 of dating Eric.

"Are you falling in love with him, do you think?" Dee questions me for what feels like the millionth time today, pausing midway through her sentence to take a bite of her egg roll.

"God I hope not. It isn't going to last, you know that."

"Yeah, well it isn't like you two aren't getting a little bit serious. He's basically been following you around for the last week. He's falling for you. I don't understand why you can't just tell your brother and be happy. When two people, like you and

Eric, can't stay away from each other, it usually means they shouldn't be apart." She tells me, offering me the last bite of her egg roll, which I gladly take as she continues to lecture me.

"Sometimes it just doesn't work out that way. You know, my mom had me when she was twenty years old, she and my dad were high school sweethearts. They had Caleb at seventeen and my mom barely made it through high school." I explain, eliciting a sigh from her. "They got married when they were freshly eighteen, and you know what happened to them? After the end of their whirlwind romance, my father left us. I can't risk everything for a young love like they did."

"Your brother will understand, Aurora. I'm not telling you to marry him, I'm telling you that you should stop forcing yourself to keep him at arm's length."

"Maybe some distance is what we need, though. We've been spending so much time together, we're going to fall in love and I don't think I can handle it." I explain, though she only shakes her head.

"Well, I'm betting on you two falling completely head over heels in love and not being able to walk away and having steamy, *steamy* sex as often as you possibly can."

"That won't be happening."

"You'd better mean the first part. If you don't tap that, Rora, I'm gonna kill you." She jokes as the back of my neck begins to tinge red to match the rest of my face.

~ ☾ ~

Day 9 of dating Eric.

I can't stop myself from smiling as I jump off of the swing, nearly falling on my face as he immediately sweeps his arms around my stomach to stop my abrupt descent.

"You're such a clutz." He tells me through a large grin as I pull out my camera, snapping a picture of our smiling faces. It only takes photos one way, so we can't see what we're doing in the slightest, but it doesn't matter. I've promised myself over and over again that if we don't work out, I'll bury the camera in a closet somewhere; I won't bother to print out the photos at all, but I know I won't be able to stop myself. I'm going to have to print them and pin them up somewhere or something.

I can't help myself 'cause in some ways, Dee was right. I'm not going to be able to stop myself from falling for him, and it's going to break my heart in the end, but it won't work out that way no matter what I want. I know my family, I know my luck, and I know it isn't going to work out in my favor. If I'm lucky enough, we'll just part ways and I'll have to deal with the heartbreak on its own.

If it doesn't, I'll have to deal with my brother.

And that's the scenario that makes me want to panic, but it's also what makes me feel like I did that night with my english professor. *Alive*.

~ (~

Day 12 of dating Eric.

I'm falling for him, I really am. It's torturous to be away from him, though being back to classes and gearing up for finals is pulling us apart for the moment. I had to skip lunch with him yesterday, and he had to skip today, so tonight is the first time I'm getting to see him for a while.

And the second I realized I missed him this morning, I got on the get-rid-of-my-feelings-for-Eric train.

I can't fall in love with him. I just can't do it.

So, I invited him over for a movie at the dorm. Where Dee is. All of the time, lately, since her girlfriend broke up with her three days ago.

Which is important, because she's been very, *very* teary ever since. She's still in that one stage of grief where she just won't stop crying and watching *10 Things I Hate About You*.

Which means a break from worrying about falling in love with my brother's best friend. It also means a break from feeling anxious about finals, *and* worrying about my roommate.

My roommate, who, for some reason, won't stop watching one scene over and over again.

So then this is what is going to happen. I'm going to wear a massive shirt and sweatpants and I'm going to put my hair up in a messy bun because when they do that in the movies, it's always when they're trying to distance themselves from something. I'm going to put on Dirty Dancing and Dee is going to rest her head on my shoulder like she has the last few nights in a row.

Except when I go to open the door, Eric is dressed in his own sweatpants and a big baggy jacket with his hair falling in his eyes just a bit, which he shoves back as he walks inside.

"I've missed you." He tells me with a grin, pulling me to his chest tightly and laying a kiss on the tip of my nose. Quickly, I pull away, making my way towards where I know Dee is waiting for me on the couch.

Or where she should be waiting for me on the couch, but where she's actually sitting and pulling on her favorite sparkly high heels.

"What's going on? I thought you were–?"

"Depressed? Yeah, I've moved on. I'm going out with that chick from my math class. Madeline and I are *done-zo*."

"Yeah? Well, uh–"

"Just stay here and chill with your boo, honey, I'll be back by two."

"It's a school night." I deadpan, though she just rolls her eyes.

"Okay, *Mom.*"

14

Eric

Watching her pull up the movie on the absolutely tiny little TV she's got in her dorm, I can't help but wish I could tell what's going through her head sometimes. She's got to be thinking of something important, with her bottom lip held between her slightly crooked teeth and her foot tapping anxiously on the ground. I'd tried to help her out as soon as I got here, but she just sat me down on the couch and got to work preparing some snacks and pulling up the movie.

It's been a couple of days since I saw her last and I can already tell that she's been having a rough week. Her eyes are ringed in red and her nails are bitten down, a habit she'd picked up in high school. I used to catch her biting them all the time around exams, but I thought she'd gotten over it a long time ago. That doesn't seem to be the case.

She's anxious. It isn't particularly hard to recognize it anymore, the little movements she makes, the little grumbles. She isn't that hard for me to read anymore, that's for sure.

And I hate it, in a way. It used to be that I couldn't tell, and maybe that was easier, really. Maybe it was easier just not to know, to just watch her and wonder, because even if I can tell what she's feeling, her thoughts are and always will be a complete and utter mystery to me.

So yeah, it's probably easier not to know, but I just pull her back against me quietly, taking her hand away from her lips where she'd been chewing on her pointer-nail.

"What's going on in that head of yours? Why are you upset?"

She takes a deep breath, shuttering against my chest.

"It's nothing, I'm not upset. Just finals and stuff." She mutters, though her head falls back against my shoulder and I watch as she blinks back tears, which she doesn't seem to realize I can see.

"You know, somehow, I don't think you're telling me the truth right now."

"Of course I am." She says as though I'm crazy for even thinking such a thing, but her voice wavers.

"No, you're not. You're thinking about something bad and it's freaking you out. Tell me what's wrong. You can tell me anything, you know that, right?"

She takes another deep breath, looking up at the ceiling as she speaks. "I'm afraid I'm going to fall in love with you."

Not quite what I was expecting, but the tear that runs down her cheek makes me think that this is a really big deal for her.

"Would that really be so bad, Aurora? Falling in love with me?"

"He'd make me choose. Caleb, he'd make me choose between you and him, and I don't think I could ever forgive myself if I ruined your relationship with him. I mean, this was just easier when we were only fooling around, but there are feelings involved here, and not just ours. Caleb, he would kill us if he ever found out about this."

"I know, I know. How about this? If you end up falling in love with me, tell me and we'll figure it out then. There's no use in stressing about something that might not even happen." I tell her— though deep down, I have those same fears swimming around my gut, threatening to overtake me. But I know I'm right, there's no use in thinking about this when it isn't even for sure yet. For all we know, that will never happen and she'll hate me by the end of this.

She calms down pretty quickly as I kiss away her tears, pulling her onto the couch with me where we eat pretzels and watch *Dirty Dancing*, which I know just happens to be one of her least favorite movies in the world, so I'm not sure why she'd chosen it.

I don't push it though. I just hold her tightly, because I know that in a month and two weeks, we'll be apart again.

And… maybe I'm a little scared too– that I'll fall in love with her and that I'll have to choose between her and Caleb; between my best friend and the girl I love.

Hell, I'm already falling for her, but she's right.

Neither of us want to admit it, but we both know that this can only end one of two ways.

We hurt ourselves or we hurt Caleb, and both ways suck.

~ (~

I wake up to the sound of her banging around in the kitchen in my apartment a couple days later, having slept over the night before– well, sort of slept over. She slept in my bed and I slept on the couch.

She promised me she'd make the pancakes she used to make when we were little, these disgusting little burnt up hockey puck pancakes that she'd cover in cinnamon and sugar to hide the flavor of burnt flour.

I'm pretty sure my family's dog is the only one who could stand eating them, but I couldn't tell her that.

I'm not sure how I'm going to get away with not eating them today, though.

So I just sit at a bar stool, watching her dance around my kitchen without music, mixing up pancake batter and turning the stove fan as far up as she can before overcooking her first pancake. I just barely remembered to take the batteries out of the smoke detectors before I went to sleep last night, though I'm glad I did, because I'm pretty sure they would already be going off if I hadn't.

"How'd ya sleep, princess?" I ask her after a moment of thought, sipping my coffee and enjoying the warm bitter taste as she flips a very burnt pancake before turning to look at me.

"Your bed is really comfy." She tells me with a smile, leaning over the counter to peck me on the lips before turning to flip her smoking pancake again. "This one's a little burnt." She adds on, putting it on top of her stack of smoking hockey pucks.

"I'm sure it'll still taste great." I assure her, grimacing slightly at the thought when she turns around to grab the syrup from the fridge, putting both on the table. We sit side by side at the little wooden card table that Caleb and I have been calling our dinner table since we moved in. She automatically sits in the chair closest to the door, the same way her brother always does, though I don't mention that to her as she digs into her first pancake, having to chew way longer than one should ever need to chew on a pancake.

"So what do you want to do today?"

"I don't know, I kinda just want to relax." She tells me honestly, looking up at me sheepishly, though she smiles at the thought of just staying home.

"Okay. We'll stay here and hang out, maybe watch *Grease*."

She loves *Grease*, it's her favorite movie.

~ (~

"What's your favorite color?" She asks me with a bright smile, resting her chin on her hand on my chest, looking up at me through her lashes with a grin on her pretty face.

"Black. What's your favorite band?"

"Cage the Elephant. What's your favorite word?"

"Aurora." I say without thinking, watching in awe as her cheeks redden and she moves up to kiss me gently. "What's your favorite place back home?"

"The pier. I like that you can see so far down the coast from the end of it. What's your favorite… animal?"

"Frog. What's your favorite utensil?"

"My favorite utensil?" She questions, quirking a brow at me. "Uh… Spork. They're so versatile."

"I'm sorry but I don't think I can be with you anymore." I tell her jokingly, turning away from her indignantly. "That is the only wrong answer to my question. How can your favorite utensil be a spork? The answer is obviously a simple spoon, Aurora."

"Well I'm sorry, I wasn't aware you had such harsh opinions on sporks. I, for one, think sporks are entertaining. They make me laugh."

"Well, that's the wrong answer. I'm so sorry, but I think I must ask you to vacate the premises. I don't think I can have a spork-lover cuddling with me."

"I'm sorry, what we're doing right now is called snuggling!" She nearly shouts, giggling as I roll her over. She tries to tickle me, though she doesn't get the chance as I accidentally roll right off the edge of the bed.

~ (~

Within moments of holding her close to me, I know that she is entirely correct on one thing. There is absolutely no way in hell we're going to get through this without falling in love with each other— without breaking our hearts.

So I'll prepare myself. I'll prepare myself to live the rest of my life, however short that may be, missing her.

Because I won't be able to stop myself from falling for her. It isn't going to happen, it isn't possible, because I'm already too deep.

She shifts silently in her sleep, nuzzling her face into my chest. My arms are wound tightly around her shoulders, her legs tangling with mine at the end of the couch. Grease plays quietly from the television, Sandy singing a song that I would normally hate to even know exists, but the fact that she loves it makes it a bit less annoying.

Hell, I think I'm already falling in love with her. It's only been a few weeks and I'm already falling in too deep for comfort.

~ (~

"So, what's her name?" Aiden questions me after a moment of thought, watching me drink my coffee a few days later. I'd just barely caught sight of her through the window of the coffee shop as she made her way to class a few minutes ago, though the very sight of her made me happier than I'd ever care to admit.

"Aurora."

"Aurora…?" He questions, looking for a last name and frowning when I make no move to elaborate any further. "Do you like her? Like, you know, really like?" He asks, making an obscene gesture with his hands, though he lowers them immediately when I make a move to smack them down.

"Stop it."

"Well, do you? She's cute but not really your usual type. I thought you liked blondes. Like Jezebel, what happened to her?" He offers up rudely, hand moving through his dark hair.

"Nothing. Nothing happened with Jezebel."

"Well maybe try with her before you go after ol' purple hair, alright?"

An aggravated sigh leaves my lungs without permission as I tell him to just drink his coffee and shut up. Thankfully, he does as he's told, pulling out his sketchbook and woofing down the last of his hot coffee.

Sometimes I regret making friends with all of Caleb's friends, though Aiden is usually the only one I don't end up hating every time I spend time with him.

15

Aurora

$\mathcal{I}$t's been three weeks now. Almost a month of being with

him— of being with a boy I am falling completely in love with every second of every day, and it feels like just yesterday we were fighting about his stupid comment on my naivety. I shouldn't be thinking about this.

I know he was right. I think he probably still is, actually, though there's no point in trying to change something like that when there's nothing I can do about it. At least, that's what I keep telling myself whenever I see the look on his face when he sees me between classes. The way he punches his friend's arms when they say something to me that I often don't actually understand.

Is it too much to ask that one of them just tells me the truth sometimes? All I want is for someone to look at me and tell me that it isn't going to work out and I'm not his normal type and he could never really fall for me, he's just wasting time and he'll be moving on in a month, when my brother gets back.

That's all I really want right now. For someone to just tell me the truth, that it isn't going to work out and that I should stop getting my hopes up.

That's what I wish he'd have told me a week ago when I told him I thought I'd fall in love with him by the end of this. I wish he'd told me that it'll never happen and that I should just stop trying because it isn't worth it. It isn't going to work out.

"Ms. James, please stay after class." My professor says, her voice sounding equally dreamy and rough. I've noticed that it's been sounding rougher and rougher over the months that I've been here, bleeding into her tone and making her sound more rude than I believe she intends, though it has the same effect either way.

Dee leans over and whispers a deep "OOOH" in my ear, similar to what you'd expect from a middle schooler in this situation. Luckily, Professor Jean doesn't hear her, or she'd be in deep shit.

I've only ever truly loved to take one class. All through high school, I hated myself, and I hated everyone else and I hated my classes and my father and my life. Now here I am, better in so many ways but also… worse off.

When I came here, I couldn't handle my life alone. I thought I was going to fail, but I haven't. I've done pretty damn well for myself and I still can't help but wish for something else to come from this. Something outside of just… okay.

I want to live the life I dreamt of from the age of seven. I want to study literature and learn the mechanisms of emotion and figure out who I am. I want to write and I want to live, but I can't, because I'll always be holding myself back in some way.

I walk up to my professor slowly, finding very quickly that she's busy looking through papers and likely doesn't want to be interrupted, but Dee is waiting for me outside so I clear my throat, trying to get her attention. She glances up at me immediately, grunting out her acknowledgement of my presence. "I was wondering how it's been going here, with you. In all honesty, I never thought I would see you again, though it seems the universe would like to keep you in my presence a bit longer than expected. Have you found the thing that makes you feel alive?"

"It isn't what makes me feel alive that's the issue. It's what doesn't make me feel alive." I explain, though I'm not sure why I'm entertaining this conversation in the first place. I'm still not really over the oddly cryptic message she gave me so long ago, it's difficult to get right back to it like this.

Though I suppose it's been a while, and to be honest, that night was the first time I've felt alive in a really long time.

But… I also know what makes me feel alive. I've always known what makes me feel alive, the rush of figuring something out, of making someone feel something with my writing. It's what I've loved to do since I was a little kid, but it's always been on the back burner.

"Well then, I'd work on figuring out how to get rid of that."

"It isn't that easy. It's never been that easy."

~ ☾ ~

"What's going on with you?" Dee questions me as we sit down in the dining hall for dinner that night, each of us stuck in our own head in some way or another, though she seems to be a lot more concerned about me than I am about her.

"Nothing." I lie, though she doesn't buy it. She just gives me a frown, reaching across the table to steal a fry off of my plate.

"I hate when you lie to me. You're not very good at it." She tells me. "Now tell me what's going on. You've been acting weird all day."

"Yeah, well, I have something on my mind."

"That doesn't mean you need to bottle it all up and keep it to yourself. You're my best friend, you can talk to me." Dee says, her eyes welling up with tears as she talks.

"I just… I think I might have made a mistake, dating Eric. I think I moved into things too soon and I think if I fall in love with him, I'm going to end up getting hurt."

"Of course you are, but isn't it still worth it? To try, I mean?"

I take a deep breath, ignoring the urge to cry as we talk about this. It isn't something I've exactly expressed to anyone outside of Eric, though Dee is right, she is my best friend and I'm hers. "I don't know anymore. I don't know if what I'm doing is right or if I'm screwing up his life or my own. I can't tell if I'm falling in love with him or if this is all a massive mistake. Honestly, I just don't know what I'm doing."

"Maybe you should talk to him about this."

"I did, sort of. He just said to let him know if I do end up falling in love with him and we'll figure it out then." I explain, receiving an understanding nod from my best friend.

"Well, I for one know what it's like to fall in love with someone you don't work well with, and if that's what you're afraid of happening, maybe some distance would be good for you. On the other hand, I don't work well with Maddy because her parents are racist pricks, not because we don't love each other, so I'm not sure if this is the same sort of situation." She says, watching me furrow my brows at her in confusion. I didn't know this about her ex-girlfriend, though Maddy and I have met a few times. She's a sweet girl, pretty too. She's just Dee's type, so I never did quite understand why they didn't work out.

They met around the same time I met Gray, and they've been head over heels for each other ever since.

"Why didn't you tell me?" I question, watching her look down at her lap, sadness strewn over her beautiful features.

"You were busy, I didn't want you to worry about me."

"Dee… you know I'm never too busy for you, right?"

"Of course, It's not a big deal anyway. It's not like we were soulmates. Her family just… doesn't support her being with a black girl. It was hard enough for them to support her being a lesbian, it was just too much for them."

"Well that's bullshit. You were the best girlfriend in the world to that girl."

"Maybe that's just not enough."

"Hey, Maddy! Hey! Wait up!" I don't know what came over me when I saw the red headed girl that my best friend has fallen for on campus the next day. Honestly, I fully intended to just stick with Dee to comfort her through this, though the second I saw Maddy, I knew that I couldn't do that.

She just looks so sad.

Maddy stops immediately, turning around to face me. Her eyes are sadder than they used to be, the beautiful green seeming more dim than normal, more somber.

"Hey. Aurora, right? Dee's roommate?"

"Yeah. I just wanted to check in with you, see if you're okay." I explain awkwardly, caught off guard by her kind voice. Her eyes fill up with tears as I talk, and I nearly fall over when she gingerly wraps her arms around my waist, resting her head on my arm.

She just feels oddly kind, as in physically. She feels kind. She squeezes me slightly.

I'm a bit taller than her, though not by much. Still her head sits beside mine, her chin on my shoulder.

"I'm sorry, I just really needed that." She tells me as she pulls away, sniffling slightly. "What's up? How're you doing?"

"Not so hot, how about you? Dee told me what happened, I'm sorry you guys are going through that."

"Yeah, well, it was sort of expected. We both knew when we went into this that it would be difficult. We're already same-sex, to be bi-racial too makes it even more difficult." She explains quietly.

"I'm sorry." I say sincerely, giving her a small, comforting smile. "I'd invite you back to my place so we could watch a movie or something, but Dee is there right now. I'm not sure she wants to see you right now, I'm sorry."

"I know. I don't exactly blame her."

~ (~

That night, Dee and I slept together in her room, me on the floor with a pillow and the spare sleeping bag we've been keeping in my closet for times like these. It's almost as if heartbreak is expected for us.

She pretends she doesn't see the way I shift around in my sleep anxiously, expecting nightmares to mar my rest.

I pretend not to notice the tears that stream down her face as she goes to sleep.

We both wake up pretty early in the morning, each of us having things to do. I'm meant to be writing a paper for psychology, and she's been planning a lunch with her sister all week long.

I pull her in for a long hug before we go our separate ways for the day. She doesn't hesitate to hug me back.

Eric: Hey, do you wanna meet up for lunch or something?

Aurora: Sure. Candy's at 1?

Eric: Sounds good. See you then.

So, it isn't strange for me to get these sporadic texts from Eric about getting lunch or dinner or just a quick coffee between classes. Between finals and everything else going on in our lives, we haven't gotten the most time together over the past few weeks. Minus that first week of dating, we actually haven't seen each other more than two or three times a week.

And like Dee said, maybe that distance is good for us. Maybe the distance is for the best, it'll make it less difficult to leave him.

So that's what happens. I go to the library, write my paper, then I meet up with Eric for lunch. He kisses me on the cheek gently as we sit down at our go-to table, waiting on one of the roller-skating waitresses to come offer us drinks.

They have all of the sodas in little glass bottles here, which makes it that much better. We usually meet at Candy's for lunch when we have the chance, though it's been a few days and I've been greatly missing their grilled cheese. And his company, of course. But the grilled cheese really is amazing.

Eric orders himself a Coke and a burger, happily digging in when they arrive, almost before telling the waitress that everything looks amazing so she can leave the table. They never leave the table until they know that the food looks good. As if anyone would ever be able to tell the kind looking woman wearing a poodle skirt and roller skates– not to mention the perm that seems to be a part of their uniform –that their food is terrible.

"How're classes going? Glad to almost be done?"

"Yeah." I respond, sounding far more nonchalant than intended.

"Well, my friend is having a Christmas party in a couple weeks— Aiden. I think you met him once or twice. I was wondering if you'd like to go with me."

Of course, I nod yes, digging into my grilled cheese with a smile and washing down the bready goodness with a sip of bottled Coke. It's so much sweeter than normal Coke for some reason. It's the fucking best.

"I'm glad. It'll be Saturday before we leave for Christmas break. You should bring Dee, too."

"I'm not sure if she'll be up to it. She's having a rough time right now."

"Okay, well, let me know." He says awkwardly before switching the topic to my psych paper.

16

Aurora

"Hey, how're you doing?" I question the girl sitting beside

me on the bench outside of the library. She pulls her eyes away from her book with a jump, turning to look at me.

"You startled me!" She says, laughing at my concerned expression. "I'm okay, you?"

"Not half bad at the moment. Wanna go get coffee or something?" I ask her, receiving a nod in return before I lead her away from the library and towards a small cafe I discovered a few days back. For some reason, I can't help but be glad I came across Maddy today. She's by far one of the nicest people I've come across over the last couple of months. Not that I've actually made too many friends, given how busy I've been. Between Eric and classes, I've pretty much been booked up since the beginning of the year. I've barely even made it to a college party, which was supposed to be one of the most important experiences of the four years I'm planning on spending here.

The place is a bit crowded at this time of day, though we're seated quickly and I go up to the front to get our coffees and food.

And then we sit there and talk. She tells me about her childhood and growing up in Tennessee. Her parents are divorced, apparently, though they co-parent her, which she says is odd but okay because her parents are better off apart.

I tell her that my dad left when I was little, but we've been keeping in contact more lately. I explain that I really, truly hate that.

She tells me that she always knew she was gay, but she never told anyone other than her older brother until she came to college a year ago. She's a sophomore apparently, and she shares a calculus class with Dee, though they met in town at a little boutique Maddy works at.

I explain that I thought Dee and I were total opposites when I met her, but I've figured out that we actually have quite a bit in common.

She tells me that she hates the world sometimes. That it's stupid that she can't be with Dee, and sometimes she wishes she could just cut contact with her family and live out the rest of her days without their prejudice. That all she wants is to be happy, over everything else.

I tell her that I just want to see the world, because I hate just staying put and letting life pass me by. I tell her that I just want to feel alive, for once in my life. I tell her about the matches, about Eric and how I'm never quite sure if what we're doing is right, but how he makes me feel like fireworks are going off in my chest every single time I see him. I tell her that I'm terrified that I'm going to fall in love with him.

She tells me she's scared of the same thing. That she isn't sure if she'll survive loving Dee.

~ (~

Maddy and I actually get along a lot better than I thought we would. I can understand why Dee loves her so much, she's probably one of the sweetest people I've ever met.

Sadly, we have to part ways after a couple of hours so that she can get to a class.

I tell her that I'm thankfully done with classes for the day.

She says that she only has one more and it's her favorite, so she doesn't mind having it later in the day than most of the other classes.

We figure out that we're meant to take biology together next semester and agree to help each other study when it starts, because she's heard that it's a really difficult class. She says that that's why she put it off until sophomore year, because she was having a rough time freshman year and just couldn't handle doing it during all of that.

And then she leaves, and I feel just a little bit more alive than I did before, because I've just done something I've never done before. I just asked a girl to lunch— a girl I don't know very well —and ended up making a new friend, someone I can really relate to.

"So we're going to a party then?" Dee asks me with a smile, pulling a dress out of her absolutely packed closet. I sit perched on the edge of her bed, holding one of her pillows to my chest.

One thing I haven't done in college so far is party. I have a feeling that it'll make me feel *alive,* though I don't know for sure what it'll be like or if I'll enjoy it at all.

But Eric invited me, and he'll be there and it's organized by one of his friends and I think I'll enjoy it.

I really hope I'll enjoy it.

"Yeah, next weekend. Are you sure you can come? I know you have an exam on Monday, you really don't have to—."

"I want to. I love parties, you know that." She explains, holding up a bright pink dress to her body. It's one that would fall down to her thighs. It's nice but not too fancy, just the type of thing you'd wear to a party. "What do you think?"

I tell her that it looks great and she begins to search for a dress for me, coming up with a forest green number that reminds me greatly of something my mother would wear. I tell her immediately and she puts it back in her closet, telling me that she plans to burn it now.

I don't blame her, really. I haven't talked with my mom much since I came here, but Dee knows that we never had the best relationship.

Parties aren't exactly my thing. They never were in high school, at least. It's not as if I've had the time to be going to them much this year, but just the memories of the sweaty bodies grinding together to terrible music and my shoes sticking to a beer-coated floor in some random senior's basement It was always my least favorite thing to do— and sadly, my best friend's absolute favorite activity. There was never a single second I actually enjoyed which was spent at a high school party, and I expect college parties to be pretty much the same.

Finally, Dee decides on a mini skirt and a tank top, which I approve of despite the fact that the tank is white, mine, and likely to get spilled on tonight.

"You know, we really didn't need to do this all a week in advance." I explain as she roots through my underwear drawer, looking for a nice looking pair so that, in her words, I can 'wrap up the present for Eric'.

"Of course we do. We'll be busy this week— finals and everything."

She's not wrong. Both of us are more than a little bit freaked out about our first college finals, and the fact that we'll be busy with them all week means that Saturday is going to primarily mean sleeping in and then going to this party. Eric thankfully offered to come and get us and play chauffeur, so I don't need to worry about that part of the equation. Sadly, I don't think I'm actually going to be able to have a lot of fun at the party.

I really always hated them, though Dee insists that it will be so much more fun with her than it was with any of the friends I had back in high school. Apparently, she's a massive party animal and,— in her oh-so-humble opinion —no party is ever complete without her presence.

I guess I don't know Dee as well as I thought I did, though I'm not sure that I'm supposed to. Nothing really prepared me to live with her, and I'm not quite positive I'll ever understand why they paired us together.

But, at the same time… I adore her. I think she's one of the best human beings I've ever met, even if we have to bicker over dinner every night and she's always leaving her shoes lying around in the communal area for me to trip over.

Dee tosses me a pair of panties to wear— a surprisingly simple pair— before beginning to root through my closet for a pretty dress. She comes up with a green dress which falls down to my knees, and I surprise myself by wishing she'd picked something a little bit more revealing. I don't mind that it's a longer dress, I really don't, but I kind of wish it was a little bit more like something she'd wear.

I'm sure she'd never be caught dead in it.

And as if she's read my mind, she tosses it on the bed and continues to root through my closet, this time with renewed vigor. As she does, she begins to hum to herself awkwardly. I turn on my speaker immediately, remembering what she'd once told me about how she can't focus without music— something about her ADHD. "Would you mind if I use that green dress for my sewing class final? I need a dress to remake and I know you hate that one. Plus, I'm like completely broke."

"Yeah sure, go for it." I find myself agreeing without much thought.

"If it turns out well you can wear it for the party!" She says, closing my closet door with a sharp thud. I really do adore Dee.

~ ☾ ~

A week of finals is really not something I ever want to have to endure again. Five final exams in five days, and my brain is 100% fried. In some ways, I think it's absolutely freaking ruined me. I haven't slept in days, though the sound of Eric softly snoring on my bed across the room makes my eyes droop with sleep. I'm so incredibly tired, though I still don't have the time or lack-of-energy to sleep.

Quickly, after making sure that Eric is asleep and pointed away from me, I slip into the green dress Dee returned to me this morning. It's certainly different from the way it was before, though not so different that it doesn't fit me. She's managed to cut slits into the side that make small portions of my stomach bulge out in ways that make me nauseous, and it's far shorter than I would have expected it to be. I'd doubt it's the same dress as before if it weren't for the striking color of the fabric.

The neckline is far lower than it was before Dee got her hands on it, and while I hated the way it made me feel before, it's far worse now. I've never really wanted to remove something from my body, but the way my skin feels held between my fingers this time makes tears well in my eyes.

"Rora?" I hear from behind me as Dee steps into my room, shutting the door behind her carefully so as to avoid waking my sleeping boyfriend. Or, whatever we are.

Is Eric my boyfriend? I'm not sure if he is or not. I'm not sure if he's ever even considered it either, but the very thought of the question makes my heart beat faster. I don't like the way this is working out anymore, knowing that he's just going to drop everything the second my brother comes back and it'll all be over for us. I don't think I can handle it when he leaves. We work out so well, how can he possibly just… leave?

"Are you alright? I heard you sniffling." Dee whispers, coming over to place her soft hands on my shoulders. She doesn't seem to notice that I'm wearing the dress she made for me; she doesn't even bother to glance down on my body, she focuses on my eyes and the tears that fill them quickly.

She uses one of her thumbs to swipe a tear away from my cheek, pulling me into a tight hug, something she seems to need just as much as I do.

"Just breathe, Rora. Breathe, you're gonna be alright."

17

Aurora

It doesn't take much time for us to make it to the party, and Eric is almost immediately pulled away by friends. No one seems to notice that I'm following close behind him, which I'm partially glad for.

It's not like he's going to stay by my side.

Dee slinks off from beside me with the quick excuse of grabbing a drink, leaving me crowded against Eric's side. His hand is casually tangled in my own, though I can't help but feel like he's helping me cross the street like a child rather than holding my hand. It doesn't feel like it should, not like a loving gesture.

His shoulders are tight as he escorts me through the crowd, a hand on my elbow as if he's a member of the Secret Service protecting me from some threat. Or a petulant mother escorting a fearful child into a birthday party. His mouth is set in a stiff line as he goes to grab us a couple bottles of soda, not bothering to ask me if I'd like anything different. There are plenty of beers and margaritas scattered about and even some sort of cocktail with Swedish Fish floating in it, but I take a sip of the Coke anyway.

I've never been big into drinking— I never really had the opportunity to be, with my mom and brother breathing down my neck all of the time. I wasn't planning on drinking tonight even if I was given the option, though I would have appreciated him asking what I wanted to drink.

I, at least, would have grabbed something other than a Coke. Coke sucks, it's just watered down Pepsi.

"Are ya having fun yet?" Eric asks me as he tucks us into a corner, though it doesn't give any semblance of privacy the way I know he means for it to. It makes me feel like a fish in an aquarium. Like the ones in the lobbies of fancy restaurants that all the kids watch until the table is ready.

"Of course." I offer up half heartedly, though he doesn't seem to notice my lack of enthusiasm.

"Great…" He trails off, seemingly not knowing what else to say. "Do you mind if I go talk to a friend really quickly?"

"Sure, go for it."

And he does. I knew he would— I did tell him to, after all. I kind of wish I hadn't come to this party at all as I watch my boyfriend disappear into the crowd of people, brushing past my dancing roommate who seems to have managed to find a drink. Her normally shaky hands are calm as she holds loosely to her red Solo cup.

"Hey Aurora, long time no see!" Someone says from somewhere behind me, forcing my attention to separate from Eric's receding back. Gray stands in front of me with a pair of cups in hand, one extended to me.

Now, I'd like to say that I'm not a complete and utter idiot when it comes to parties, but I am. Even as the Dr. Pepper stings my throat on the way down, I don't pay much mind to the feeling. "Yeah. It's been awhile." I agree, though my heart certainly isn't in it. I can't focus on much outside of the blasting music. Tears prick at my eyes, but I prod them back as soon as they come.

"Well how've you been?" He asks, a spark of something dangerous in his eyes. You wouldn't know it from looking at him, but Gray seems to have something in him I never noticed before.

Something I don't like… at all.

"I've been fine, Gray." I answer simply, downing the last few drops of the Dr. Pepper he gave me. I don't know where my Coke is anymore. The small plastic bottle is nowhere to be found.

"I'm glad. Do you want another soda?" I give a nod, not really trusting my voice anymore. I'm not sure if I can trust my hands not to shake as I hand him the empty cup, ignoring the small amount of blue residue in the bottom. I barely even notice the stuff, though I'm pretty sure I'll regret it later.

I'll definitely regret it later.

Gray saunters off back into the crowd, though I barely notice that he's left. My head spins slightly as I turn to lean my forehead against the cool wall, hoping it'll dull the headache brought on by the blaring music being played. Everyone seems to be jumping slightly off beat, making the floor vibrate beneath my feet uncomfortably. Gray doesn't come back to me, despite me wishing he had as soon as my throat begins to ache uncomfortably.

Something's wrong. Something's very wrong.

"Hey, watch it!" Someone shouts as they bump against my shoulder. I can feel my organs rattling around in my chest and stomach. My head pounds to the beat of the techno music, my eyes straining to see a man dancing on a table across the room. My toes curl against the soles of the uncomfortable shoes Dee had lent me for the purpose of this idiotic party. Someone thrusts a beer into my hand, the cold bottle stinging my palm.

I barely manage to stop myself from dropping it. Someone— or something —pushes it up to my lips, the sticky, cold liquid flowing down my throat. It does nothing to stop the pain, to keep me right side up, and I end up on the ground. No one seems to notice as they continue to dance around my shrunken body. Someone steps on my hand, forcing a pained hiss from my lips.

A second beer is added to the pool of fear in my stomach. People just keep handing them to me, and I no longer remember where I am. The aquarium-corner is long gone at this point, and my hand stings. Someone shouts something about blood in my ear, but I can't pay them any attention. I wish I could— it feels rude not to —but I just can't focus long enough to reply. I wipe my hand on the front of my dress, grabbing a half-empty margarita from the table beside me. Someone grumbles at me and someone else jostles roughly against my side as I gulp down the icy tart liquid.

Words whisper against the back of my throat, but they can't seem to release themselves from my clenched teeth.

I don't remember how I got here. I don't know where I'm going. All I know is the pain that seems to be flowing through me.

Something smacks roughly against my temple, stinging my eye as everyone keeps swaying along to the music around me.

They don't seem to notice the hot, sticky feeling that's taking over my face. They don't seem to have that problem.

Somewhere across the room, people begin to chant as a man is forced into a handstand on top of a keg— or maybe it's right next to me.

Someone pulls me away from the crowd into a bright bathroom, dabbing a wet cloth against my face. "What the hell happened to you, peach?" They grunt, trying to hold my stinging hand still in their own as I try to wriggle away from the wet cloth.

I try to say something, but the words don't come out.

"Come on peach, stay with me." The person says, grabbing hold of my cheeks as my eyes begin to close. "You're gonna be okay. Just keep your eyes open. Keep your eyes open, peach."

I don't do as I'm told, making the figure curse. My head lulls onto his shoulder without my permission, though I don't do anything to stop it.

"Come on, peach, you gotta drink some water." He insists, holding a glass to my lips. I don't know whether or not I actually drank any of it by the time he pulls it away from me, but I also can't find the energy to care. "We gotta get you outta here, peach. You're not lookin' so hot."

"I'm always hot." I slur against my own wishes, feeling the stinging sensation begin to return to my throat. It feels as if I've drunk fire.

Or possibly Fireball. I'm not sure.

"'Course ya are. I'll be right back, peach, just stay here." And before I know it, the warmth is gone and the light feels too bright. My hand feels tight and broken, like a rubber band that's sat around for too long. Like if I pull just a little bit, my whole hand will snap. Or maybe my life will.

My breath speeds up and I feel like I'm suffocating. I barely manage to yank the zipper down my back and remove my arms from the straps, letting it slip down revealing the plain gray bra I'd ended up wearing beneath it.

It had made me feel undesirable when I realized it was the only good bra I had to wear beneath such a pretty dress, though now I don't mind it.

I don't know how or why I end up on my feet, making my way across the hall to a random bedroom. I don't know how or when I manage to spot Eric amongst the four or five people hanging out in there, but he seems to notice me pretty quickly.

"Er—ic?" I stutter, hiccuping in the middle of his name and drawing his attention to me as I sit down on the bed beside him. His friends look at me in some form of horror and shock, one of them letting out a small scream, though I'm not sure why.

"What happened to you, Rora?" He questions, pulling me into his lap gently and bringing his lips lightly to mine, tasting my lips for alcohol. He moves immediately when I push him back by his cheek, not paying much attention to what's going on around me as I slump down against his shoulder gently. "Who did this to you, honey?"

Before I can even begin to think about an answer— which, admittedly, took me a little longer than normal to get to —the door to the room bursts open once again.

"peach, I told you to stay put! You scared the shit outta me!" The man from before shouts at me from the doorway, making his way over to me immediately. "We gotta go to the hospital, peach."

"What the fuck are you doing here?!" Eric shouts at the man, making my ears hurt as I move myself from his lap. Someone else grabs onto my shoulders and I end up laid over someone's bare legs, hands tangled in my own as I worry my metalic-tasting lip between my teeth. I can barely see Eric standing to confront the man. "What did you do to her?!"

"As if, jackass! I found her like this. Did you really fucking drug her? I thought you were a douchebag before, but this is a whole new level!"

"I'll call the fuckin' cops on you right now, man. What did you do to her?" Eric seethes.

"I'll fucking kill you if you've hurt her." The other man insists, seeming to have not even heard the question he was asked. He doesn't seem to care, either.

"You two idiots need to shut up. She's bleeding and she's drugged, she needs to go to the hospital. I'm driving, you two can follow in a different car." Someone says, and a pair of strong arms reaches beneath my knees and armpits, lifting me into the air. People bump up against my arms and legs as we make our way through the crowded party. The music stings my ears worse than before, making me bury my head in my chauffeur's neck. I can't help the tears that trickle down my face, nor the blood that seeps along with them. I can barely discern the red stains on my green dress from the way it's bunched just above my breasts, the back still completely unzipped.

I'm placed in the backseat of a car, my head resting on someone's lap. A hand is once again placed in mine. The radio plays almost silently as the car lurches forward.

The lights outside of the car are bright and flashing as we speed into town.

18

Eric

$\mathscr{T}$he hospital my friends decided to take her to is brightly

lit and smells of blood and bleach, a mixture I can't even pretend doesn't make me nauseous.

"I'm sorry, Mr. McForse, but I can't let you see the patient unless you're related. Please, just sit down and the doctor will see you soon. She's most likely suffering from alcohol poisoning." Jase huffs at the response from the nurse, making his way back to his seat. He doesn't sit with the rest of us, my friends having selected to keep their distance.

Maddy is making a last ditch effort to wipe Aurora's blood from her thighs, where she'd rested her head the whole way to the hospital. There's a large red splotch still present, and it feels to me like it's burned into my brain. Like it was on my very own body.

The girl ties her black hair up into a ponytail on the top of her head before returning to her work, trying to make the red disappear.

David sits beside her, staring down at his hands as if he's ashamed of something. Or perhaps he's praying.

And finally, Aidan stands leaned up against a wall. He's never met her before, but he's certainly the most anxious about what's happening. Well, outside of Jase.

Within a few hours, a woman in a white coat exits the ER. Jase is on his feet almost immediately— though I'm faster.

"I'm sorry to have to tell you all this, but Aurora was drugged tonight. We've tested her blood, and she seems to have been given a near-lethal dose of Rohypnol. She's very lucky to have survived it."

"But she'll be okay, right?" I question, my hands bunching into fists at my sides. Tears prick at my eyes painfully, but I push them away, ignoring the sting.

"Yes, she'll be alright." The doctor says hesitantly, "But the toll this will take on her mentally could be extreme. Her injuries are rather extensive. She seems to have been trampled, kicked, and even force-fed. She's agreed to see visitors, but I must insist that neither of you boys go in to see her." She says, glancing down at her feet as she directs the comment to Jase and I. "Until we can prove she wasn't assaulted, I can't let either of you in. I've been informed that you've been accusing each other of drugging Ms. James."

"Fine. Maddy, could you just make sure she's okay? I have to make some calls." I offer up, watching my friend slink behind the doctor into the Emergency Room, disappearing behind the heavy metal doors and around a corner.

"Who are you going to call?" Aidan questions, though I find myself too distracted to answer him as I sort through my contact list, trying to find Dee. She answers on the first ring, her worried voice filling my ears.

"Where did you go?!" She screeches through the phone. The background is quiet and I can just barely hear the breeze outside of her window, the traffic down the street beside her and Rora's dorm.

"We're at the hospital, Rora was drugged. They won't let me see her until they're sure she wasn't assaulted. Do you think you could come down here? I think they might call the police on me, and I need someone I trust here to take care of her."

"She was fucking drugged? Of course, I'll be there in half an hour. And Eric, I swear to god, if you hurt her—."

I don't catch the end of her threat as I pull the phone away from my ear and hang up, pulling up a different contact.

There are only so many options when it comes to Aurora's family. I know I should call Caleb, that he'd want to know about this. If it were my sister I'd want to know.

But I don't have it in me to call him. And her mom won't be any help anyways, so I end up calling Aurora's least favorite family member.

Joseph Murtery does not pick up on the first ring.

Or the second.

Or the third.

Joseph Murtery picks up the third time I call him. His voice is gruff and tired as he makes a half-hearted threat, though he sharpens up the second I tell him what's happened.

I'm on the phone with him as he books a flight, as Maddy comes back into the waiting room with tears running down her face. I watch as Aidan pulls her into a tight hug. David pulls a cross from beneath his t-shirt, holding it to his forehead as he prays.

"I'll be there in three hours." Joseph finally says, hanging up the phone without saying goodbye.

"Maddy?" I question, taking a seat beside my friend. I find myself glancing over at Jase briefly, finding that he's talking to someone, speaking gruffly into his phone.

"They're running a rape kit, Eric. She's not doing great."

~ ☾ ~

Before I know it, the waiting room begins to fill up. Jase is joined by a few other people our age, though I don't recognize any of them. All three are girls, each with some sort of tattoo or piercing. Joseph shows up earlier than expected, rushing immediately to check on his daughter— and how much the hospital stay is going to cost him.

Dee chooses to sit away from everyone, sending glares at me every few minutes before returning to her phone. I only return to my own, scrolling through the thousands of search results about how Rape Kits work. From what I'm gathering, they're absolutely awful.

Part of me wants to cry for her, for the girl I've begun to fall in love with. The other part just wants to die.

I knew she'd never been to a party like this. I knew she never really wanted to come, that she was doing it for me.

I shouldn't have left her alone. I went and looked for her but she was gone, and I should never have given up. I shouldn't have assumed she was with her roommate, I should've made sure.

She's my everything, and she could have died tonight. I'm not sure what I would have done if she had.

After several more hours, the doctor once again stands before us all. It's the first time every single one of us has managed to stand beside each other without wanting to kill each other.

"So, thankfully the rape kit came up negative. We also tested her blood to try and trace the Rohypnol, but it seems to be a common form. I'm sorry, but it's unlikely the police will be able to catch the person who did this. I do recommend that Ms. James file a police report, though. Now, as for her health: she's doing fine. Her blood pressure is normal and her wounds have stopped bleeding completely. I'm going to send her home with antibiotics for her wounds, but other than the cast, that's about all I can do."

"The cast?" Jase questions, barely before me.

"Yes. Ms. James sustained a hairline fracture to her wrist when she was stepped on. It should heal up fine within the next few weeks, but I have put her in a cast just to be safe. Also, someone will need to stay with her— awake —for the next 24 hours. Because of the amount of Rohypnol in her bloodstream, we recommend that she stay conscious for as long as possible.

"Can I see her now?" I ask the woman. I can hear the drowsiness of my voice, the way it wavers. She nods immediately.

"She's requesting your company, actually. You're all clear to see her. She's in room 229, first door on the right down that hallway.

I don't listen to the last of her explanation as I storm through the doors of the ER, doing exactly what I've wanted to do for the last few hours. I just want to see her, to hold her if she'll let me.

She looks so fragile in that sterile-looking white bed, though her eyes are bright as she watches the muted TV mounted on the wall in front of her. I take the seat beside her bed silently, waiting for her to say something.

"The kit came up negative. No one touched me." She says quietly, her voice cracking with every syllable.

"I know, the doctor told me." Her eyes shut tightly as she reaches over to grab my hand.

"They said they probably won't be able to prosecute for it. Even though I know who it was, they said I don't have the evidence."

I don't ask who she's talking about. Not yet, at least.

I want to be here for her right now, and I can't do that if she tells me who did this to her. I won't be able to stay with her if I know who hurt her.

I watch as her face seems to soften, her eyes remaining shut but her eyelashes fluttering a bit. She's getting ready to fall asleep.

"I'm sorry, sweetheart, but I can't let you go to sleep right now." I tell her, pressing a kiss to her forehead and grabbing the remote for her bed, raising the back up so she's sitting mostly upright. She groans softly, clearly a tad bit annoyed with me. She squints her eyes open against the bright lights of the hospital room.

I've never seen her so obviously scared before in my life. Not when she went into surgery to get her appendix removed, not when she fell off her bike for the first time. Not even when her dad left for the last time. She's terrified.

"Could you hold my hand? Please?" She begs, startling me slightly. I tangle my fingers with her unharmed ones immediately, though it doesn't seem to be what she's looking for. She doesn't say anything more, just holding tightly to my hand. The others come and go throughout the night, and the doctors prepare her for release. She can barely walk, so they place her in a wheelchair sometime around sunrise, and they wheel her out to my car. She doesn't seem to even realize she's being buckled into my passenger seat, and her head lulls back against the headrest as if she can't hold it up any longer.

We make it back to the apartment quickly and she slumps down on the couch, her back against the armrest. I rush to grab a blanket from my bed when I see her shoulders begin to shake, laying it over her legs. A tear runs down her face, but she tries to hide it from me so I don't mention it to her.

Throughout the night she manages to drink a few glasses of water and down way more than the allotted amount of Ibuprofen. I don't know if she's okay— I seriously doubt she is, but she doesn't say a word to me all night long. She keeps the television on mute and she doesn't even attempt to go to sleep. She just keeps staring at her hands, as though she expects them to stop acting as her own. As if she thinks that they hate her, that they have a murderous mind of their own.

I hate seeing her like this. She looks hollow, as though she thinks she isn't the same anymore. She isn't wearing a smile or even her small frown that she always has when she thinks really hard. She isn't who she was before this happened, and I can't help but blame myself. I can't help but think that it's all my fault.

I walked away from her last night. I walked away just like I have to do in a month when her brother comes back. I don't know how I'll do it, how I'll be able to leave her like we had planned. All I'll have left is the cruddy little painted camera she gave me. I'm going to have to walk away from her, and I won't be able to care about it, not with Caleb around to watch over her.

I'm going to have to leave her.

19

Aurora

The hospital room they've put me in is bright and sterile-

looking, more so than the hospitals I've been in before— which, let's be honest, is probably a good thing. The nurse I'm given is a rather severe man with a clean-shaven face, and he manages to place the I.V. in my arm on the first try, which I'm thankful for. One of the things I've always hated most is how queasy I feel when I'm around needles. He thrusts a juice box into my hand and leaves the room without saying a word to me.

I don't think about what happened to me. I don't think at all. I don't want to think or feel or do anything. I don't want to think.

Not anymore.

People come and go. People I know and people I don't. They ask me if they can do anything to help me, if they can get me anything. They say things to me that I can't think about. A doctor asks me if I consent to having a rape kit done.

I do. I don't know if I was assaulted or not. I don't remember.

They maneuver my body for me. They don't ask me questions like I expected them to, and they figure out that I wasn't assaulted pretty quickly. They leave me alone.

It doesn't feel better. I thought it would feel better to be alone, to know I wasn't assaulted.

Or maybe I was. I don't really know for certain if what he did to me is considered assault. I don't want to think that it is, but I also don't want to think that it isn't.

Someone comes to put a cast on my hand. She asks me if it hurts but I don't have the energy to answer her. I don't know if it hurts anyways. She tells me I'm brave, but I don't agree.

She leaves. They let Eric in eventually. He sits beside me until I can gather the words I'm looking for.

He holds my hand when I ask him to. It's impersonal, just like it was before. I don't say anything more. He sits with me all night, making sure I stay awake. He tries to start a conversation but I just can't seem to pay attention to it, no matter how hard I try to. He doesn't seem to mind, though. Eventually his thumb begins to stroke over my bruised knuckles, and I feel the small spark of romance I was hoping for earlier at the party.

I ask him how long he's been here. He doesn't have an answer, he says he doesn't know what time it is. There isn't a clock in this room. I think they should add one, just to be helpful. But at the same time, I'd have to know how long I've been here if they had a clock, and I don't want that.

The doctor brings me a clipboard with a stack of paper, the word DISCHARGE written in big red letters on the top. I fill it out quickly and they help me into a wheelchair. I can't really walk yet. They say it'll take a little while, that I shouldn't push myself to do anything I'm not ready for.

I wasn't ready to be in the hospital, but I wasn't given a choice.

I wasn't ready for any of this.

They remind me to stay awake— that I have to stay awake no matter how much I want to sleep. That they can't let me go home unless I promise them I'll try to stay awake. They help buckle me into Eric's car, and my head rests against the seat. I can't keep it up very well. I don't even really try to. I want to sleep— or maybe I want something different. I want to rest. I want to close my eyes and not have to think. No nightmares, no insomnia. I just want to rest.

Eric drives us back to his apartment with the radio off. It's the first time I've ever been in his car without the music blaring. He told me he can't focus without it, though I guess this is an extraneous circumstance because he doesn't seem to mind the quiet. He has a white-knuckled grip on the steering wheel all the way back. He helps me flop down on his couch and gets me a blanket. He sits at the other end of the couch with my feet in his lap all through the night. He doesn't seem to mind staying awake with me.

I don't know if I would mind if I were in his place.

Eric Meridian is my favorite person. I know that for sure, now. I hate him because I can't hate him. Because no matter what happened to me, I can't be upset with him. I can't let myself blame him for what happened. I can't yell at him for leaving me alone, or for focusing on beating up Jase instead of getting me to the hospital. I can't hate him no matter how much I want to, because even when I'm angry, he's right there helping me. He rests with me the whole day after my 24 hours awake are up. He stays in bed with me sleeping, holding me tightly and making me feel safer than I ever felt in that hospital— than I've ever felt in my dorm room. Maybe even safer than I felt at home as a kid.

He wards off the nightmares that threaten my sleep, and he makes it so I can… rest. He lets me rest.

I want to hate him so badly. I want to blame him for what happened, but I can't. I try to and I fail.

I don't have someone to blame for this. I want to be able to blame someone, but there's only one person at fault, and there isn't anything I can do about it. There isn't anything I can do even though I know who it was.

~ (~

I remember the dancing people, all moving around me, bumping against me. I remember the look of fear on Eric's face when he saw me. I remember everything. I remember everything and I remember nothing at the same time.

I remember Gray's sickly sweet smile as he handed me the drink. I'm sure he knew what was in it. Perhaps he put it there himself, though I'm not quite sure why. I don't really care either, I only care that it happened in the first place. That he did this to me.

My dorm room is exactly how I left it before the party, but it feels different for some reason. It doesn't feel like *my* room anymore, it feels like someone else's. It feels like it doesn't belong to me. It hasn't felt like my own since it happened. *I* haven't felt like my own since it happened. It's like I don't have control of myself anymore. I don't have control of my brain or my body or my feelings. I can't sleep, I can't think.

It's been ages since it happened. Weeks have gone by since I was in that hell, and yet I can't seem to get over it. I can't get over the fact that I couldn't control my own body.

I filed a police report, but they couldn't do anything for me. Not when there was no evidence Gray was the one who did it. Other than my memories, of course. But who cares about my memories when Gray Anderson is an 'Upstanding Member of the Community'. Not when his parents are richer than Midas. Everything they touch turns to gold and everything he touches turns to coal. He's a terrible person, but it doesn't matter because he's rich— and because he's a man.

Since the accident, Eric has managed to find time to eat lunch with me every single day. I think he thinks Gray will try again, though I can't seem to care about his purpose in sitting with me. Not when I really really enjoy spending that time with him every day.

I don't like taking the bus. I don't like the seats that scrape against my skin or the way people are always chattering around me so that I can barely hear myself think. I don't enjoy it, not at all.

But, when it comes to Eric, I'd be willing to ride the bus a million times over. His apartment is a little bit further away from my dorm room than I'd prefer, though the fact that I have to take the bus to get there when he can't pick me up makes it worse.

I really don't like the bus. I really really don't.

Eric's apartment is a happy place for me. The whole place is just so… him, and I couldn't imagine a better place.

I think it's hard not to love him. I think I've spent so much time convincing myself I can't, I didn't even realize it was too late. It's too late not to love him because he's always been there, and I've always loved him. I've loved him since he sat beside me in the hospital ten years ago, just as much as I loved him when he sat beside me three weeks ago. I love him, and I think I was born loving him. I'll die loving him, probably.

Or maybe I'm crazy. Maybe I don't know what love is at all, but I know that he's as close as I've ever gotten. He's everything to me.

He's my version of love. He's the person I trust more than almost everyone else. He is mine and I am his. Only his.

~ ☾ ~

Eric opens the door for me quickly, ushering me inside the dull and slightly messy apartment he calls home. His lips press to mine in a sweet greeting, though he removes himself quickly.

I don't know if I want him to, though. I want him to keep kissing me, but he doesn't want to push me, clearly.

We eat dinner together on the couch, relishing in our last night together. It snuck up on me, the idea that I'd have to leave him. This is the end of it all.

We sit together on the couch, watching a movie I can barely pay attention to. He tangles his hand with mine.

His lips trail down my neck and his hand fixes itself on my thigh. "I love you, you know that, right?" He asks quietly.

"I love you too, Eric." I tell him after a moment of thought. "I love you so much."

"I'm glad. You still have your camera, right?"

"I have so many memories, it could fill a million of those crappy little cameras. I won't forget any of it."

"God, I love you so much. I love you so fucking much."

He barely manages to get his words out between kisses as he migrates up to my lips and he strips my shirt from my body.

20

Eric

"What the fuck is this?" I hear through the thin veil of

sleep, knowing the voice better than I know anything else.

Caleb stands at the end of my bed with a deep frown on his face, his cheeks turning red and his eyes widening a startling amount.

He's angry, really angry, and it takes me only a moment to figure out why, exactly.

The answer is the girl laying in my bed, head resting on my chest, deeply asleep.

"You fucked my little sister?" He questions, slightly louder than before.

"No– That's not it, Caleb–."

"You Fucked. My Little. Sister." He seethes, grabbing my arm and yanking me away from her. She begins to stir from her slumber, her eyelashes batting against her soft cheeks and making me wish more than anything that we were alone.

But we aren't. Caleb is here, and he's trying to land a punch in my gut, and I let him. I have to let him, because I did sleep with his sister, and I do regret hurting him.

I regret hurting him but I can never regret being with her. I can never regret falling in love with her.

"Caleb, stop!" She shouts over and over again, pulling my shirt over her head and trying to grab at his arms, trying to stop him from hurting me. He nearly knocks her off her feet as he shoves her away, and I immediately grab for his arms, trying to stop him.

"Stop, stop, you're hurting her!" I try, shoving him away and grabbing for her waist, trying to stop her from falling the way that I've gotten used to doing most days I see her.

She stabilizes herself on my arms, holding me tightly and looking down at the red welts all over my stomach. "Oh my god." She mutters, reaching to touch them, though Caleb grabs her away from me immediately.

"Don't touch her!" Caleb shouts at me, yanking her away from me by the arm, pulling her back towards him in a manner that looks mildly painful, which becomes clear the moment she flinches away from him.

And I see red. I see red because I remember that same flinch from the night she was drugged. It was only a few weeks ago, a month at most, and it still sits fresh in my mind. The absent, sad look in her eyes as she watched the road. The frown on her face as the police told her they couldn't do anything to prosecute the guy who hurt her— the guy who tried to kill her. I remember everything, and just the thought of it makes me angry.

"Get your hands off of her. You're hurting her!" I shout at him, though it sounds muffled to my ears.

She mutters something quietly, trying to get back to me, but Caleb holds her back. She flinches again. I try to get to her, but he punches me in the stomach again.

"You fucked my little sister! I can't believe you'd do that!"

"Don't touch her!" I shout right back at him, not acknowledging what he'd said to me. I can't, because I can't think about anything but the look of pain and sadness on her beautiful face.

"I can't believe you! You just couldn't help yourself, could you?! I trusted you!"

"Caleb! Stop!" She shouts over and over again as he lays into me, landing punch after punch into my abdomen. "I love him! I love him! Stop!" She shouts.

Caleb doesn't stop. "You don't know what love is." He seethes angrily. "You don't know what it feels like, you don't know anything about it."

I don't try to stop him from hitting me. I don't want to, so I don't try to. I know that no matter how much I love her, I deserve everything he's giving me.

This is my best friend. My best friend is laying into me, making blood drip from my nose down my chin. She's screaming and crying, trying to pull on his arm, but he doesn't stop. He doesn't even seem to notice her attempts to help me.

I deserve this.

After a while, he begins to slow down. She barely manages to get him to stop before he's standing and grabbing her wrist, pulling her into his room roughly. The last thing I hear is him shouting at her before I black out, no longer able to keep my swelling eyes open. I don't fight the feeling. I don't want to and I don't think I deserve to.

~ (~

I don't have a place to live anymore. He kicked me out of my own apartment, so I find myself struggling to find a place to sleep.

She didn't say anything as Caleb forced me out the door. She didn't try to stop him, she didn't tell him she loves me again.

She was silent. So quiet I question if she'd lost her voice yelling at him. Her hands shook furiously as she cupped her face, hiding her tear-filled eyes from me.

~ (~

The plan was simple. Two months, and then we'd end it. Everything was so well planned out, and yet it still exploded.

The camera she gave me basically burns holes in my mind no matter where I put it. I can't stop thinking about the plan we had, the intentions we worked out.

We're out of time now. It all should have ended yesterday, and yet I can't leave her now. I can't let her leave me, I just can't do it, not now that I know she loves me. Not now that everythings' gone to hell anyways. So many precautions were taken, and yet… nothing. It was all for nothing.

Caleb still found out. She's still broken hearted and my relationship with my best friend is still ruined. I wonder if there is something I could have done to make it all work out. Maybe I could have broken her heart that night, though I don't think I would have survived it.

I love her. I love her more than I love myself, more than I love anything. She's the best thing that's ever happened to me. I don't deserve her love, I know that because I never have and I never will. There's nothing about me that matches up to her, that's worth her love and affection, and yet she still gives it freely and without wanting anything in return.

I never used to believe in that kind of love. In the love that shatters hearts and makes you wonder if everything you've ever done wrong was just pushing you towards this moment in your life. I don't know if it was all worth it, but I don't regret anything.

She isn't perfect. She's nowhere close to perfect, and she'll never believe me if I tell her she is. But… in a way, her kind of perfection is exactly what I love about her. The way she dyed her hair purple unevenly and she can hardly walk without tripping over her own feet. She isn't like anyone else I've ever known, and yet… she's always been my everything. Ever since we were kids, she was my everything.

She told me once that she had a bit of a crush on me growing up. I've always wondered if that's what it was that I always felt for her, if it was a crush or if I always knew I had to love her. Maybe she knew too, or maybe she didn't. I don't think I'll ever know.

But… it doesn't matter. I love her and she loves me, and that's all that matters now. Not how Caleb will feel about it, not how it could blow up our lives. Just that we love each other. She's the best person in the world, and she's mine, and that's what matters to me. That's all that matters to me.

~ ☾ ~

Aidan snores like a chainsaw. Sleeping on his couch is like sleeping next to a revving engine, but it's the only option I have.

Aurora hasn't talked to me in days. She hasn't said a word, hasn't answered a text message or even an email.

Caleb, on the other hand, has sent me hundreds of threatening texts, each and every one promising some sort of bodily harm. It's hard to believe that it's my best friend saying those things to me.

Or… maybe he isn't still my best friend. I don't know if he is anymore.

Maybe it doesn't matter if he is or not, because I don't think he'll ever talk to me again unless it involves some sort of hostage situation. I don't deserve it either way. I don't deserve to have him around anymore, not when I betrayed his trust like I did.

But I love her, so it doesn't matter… right? I can't regret what I did because it brought me to her. Even as my stomach and face develop dark bruises, I can't regret it.

I love her so much.

~ ☾ ~

Aurora James is a menace to society. She thinks she's smarter than she really is. She's clumsy and she's lazy and every time I see her I swear she's got a new keychain attached to her bag or her keys. Half of the photos she takes of me are blurry and the one time I took her to a party turned out to be hell. She can't spell but she types faster than the speed of sound.

Aurora James is the best thing that's ever happened to me.

Dee lets me into their dorm without hesitation, knocking on her roommate's door softly. "Rora, Eric is here." She says quietly, opening the door for me when she doesn't get a response. "Just be careful. She isn't doing so great." Dee whispers to me before letting me step into the room. Aurora is sitting at her little desk typing furiously on her cruddy laptop.

Her eyes never leave the screen as she speaks to me. "What are you doing here?" She asks simply, pausing before continuing. "I thought I made it pretty clear I was avoiding you."

"I can't let you avoid me anymore." I tell her. She barely falters in her writing.

"It isn't your choice. It's mine, and it's Caleb's. We said we couldn't let this get between us and it did, I can't keep hurting him."

"Well I can't leave you. I can't let it end yet."

She pauses, her eyes squeezing shut before she briefly turns to me. "You don't have a choice in the matter. Caleb is my brother, he means far too much to me for us to ruin everything like this. He's my brother."

"And he's my best friend! Do you think I don't hate myself for this? Do you think I don't absolutely despise myself for loving you? Of course I do, but I can't help it." She takes a deep breath as I talk, her eyes filling with tears, though she still refuses to look up at me. "I tried not to love you, and I failed. I don't want to keep trying anymore. I just want to love you."

"We hurt him, Eric— badly. Is it really worth it to keep this going, knowing that it'll just keep hurting him? He trusted us and we messed it all up, why should we get to be happy if it hurts him?"

"I know, it doesn't make any sense, but I can't let it end like this. It was a mistake, saying we could let it go after two months, because we can't. I love you, and if we let this end right now, I'll never forgive myself for it. I can't let it end yet. I just can't."

"You don't have a choice!" She shouts at me, standing up quickly and spinning to face me. Tears race down her pink cheeks and drip from her chin.

"But you do! Please, Rora, I can't lose you like this." I insist. Her eyes shut tight before she whispers the words I knew she would.

"I know."

21

Aurora

$\mathscr{I}$ love him, but this… I can't let him do this. I love him so much.

But I can't let him throw away his future for me. I can't let him toss his life aside— his dreams. I just can't do it.

The letter weighs heavy in my hands as I sit on the couch in Aidan's apartment. I shouldn't have looked at it, I know that, but the big yellow rectangle on the front grabbed my attention. There were always so many of their magazines around growing up, all because of him. I would have been disappointed with myself had I not looked through the envelope.

Dear Mr. Meridian,

We are pleased to offer you the opportunity to join us on our upcoming archaelogical dig in Rome, Italy. We were very happy to receive your application and have found your resume to be very impressive. Please return the form attached to this letter to our office within the week.

Just as a reminder, this is a dig regarding human remains originating from the Renaissance period. We would greatly appreciate having your Archaeological photography skill set with this dig, as it will garner heavy publicity. Currently, we are all set to fly to Rome on **February 1st** *of this year. Any and all expenses for this trip will be carried by National Geographic, including your cellular usage and food.*

Once again, thank you for your interest and we greatly look forward to hearing back from you.

Sincerely,

Martha T. Burnstock

Head of Italian Archaeological Field Research

Sapienza University of Rome

I can barely think straight as I read through it. Again and again and again. This is his dream, it always has been. I can't imagine why he isn't at the post office right now mailing back the form. Let alone why he hasn't even filled it out.

But I'm here.

"I didn't mean for you to see that." He tells me as he walks back into his friend's living room, barely pausing when he sees what I'm reading.

"Why haven't you filled out the form?" I question, pulling it from the envelope. He hasn't even filled in his name yet.

"Because I'm not accepting the job." He says as though it's obvious, though if I had something in my mouth I would be choking. Or perhaps I would have sprayed it everywhere like they do in the movies.

"But this is basically your dream job! You're only twenty and you're turning down your dream job? Why the hell would you do that?!"

"We just got everything figured out, Rora! You just want me to pack up and leave?! The flight is in less than two weeks." He's irritated, clearly, though I don't let up on him. I have no intention of doing so until he tells me exactly why he's being so incredibly stupid. "I already lost Caleb, I can't lose you too. Not now."

"Are you stupid?! You can't turn down this job because of me! You just can't!"

"Yes, I can." He shouts right back at me.

"No, you absolutely fucking can't, Eric. I love you so much, but I can't let you do this." I tell him, though he doesn't pay me any mind. "If you don't do this, you're going to spend the rest of your life hating yourself— hating me. I watched my mom suffer for years with a man who resented her, I can't do that to myself. It's your choice if you want to go or not, but I won't be the reason why you don't."

"What are you saying?" He questions, though I can tell he's already figured it out. I think he knew the second I picked up the letter that this was going to ruin us. That there was no way this would work out for us.

Caleb is my brother, and if I ever needed my big brother to help me out, this is the time.

After helping Eric pack his bags for Italy— one of the hardest things I've ever done —I make my way over to their old apartment quickly. I don't care if he's mad at me, I don't care if he hates me for what I did.

I need my big brother, now more than ever.

He opens the door immediately, and he doesn't fight it when I rush into his arms. He just holds me.

"Eric called, he said you'd be coming here." He whispers into my hair, making tears rush to my eyes. "He said he's leaving."

"We broke up. He's going to Italy. He was offered this… absolutely incredible job, and I couldn't let him turn it down. He said he wanted to stay here, that he wanted to be with me but I told him no."

"I'm proud of you, Rora. I'm so fucking proud of you."

"But I hurt you." I say, confused.

"Yeah, but you did it for you. You did it because you fell for him, and no matter how much that pisses me off… I'm happy for you."

"But why? I dated your best friend! In secret! I completely fucked you over!"

"I love him, I do, but I love you more than anything. You matter the most to me, and no matter what, you're the one I care for most. If I had to choose one of us to fall in love like that, it would be you."

"Can I ask you something?" I ask thoughtfully, not really wanting to bring up the subject but knowing I have to.

I always knew he loved his best friend. Since we were kids, I knew that Caleb wasn't like all of the other boys his age. He didn't want to go out with the girls— he didn't even take a girl to prom.

But… all this time, did he want to be with his best friend? Does he love Eric the same way I always have?

"You love him, don't you? Like… really love him?"

"I didn't think you knew about that." He says with a sigh.

"You're my brother. You can't hide things from me, not like this. Not the stuff that matters."

"How long have you known?" He questions shyly.

"Since I was twelve, I guess. We were playing spin-the-bottle at Jamie Riche's birthday party and someone made a joke about you landing on another boy. I've never seen you so embarrassed in my life. Then at that dinner with Joseph you kept looking at him— it was like you wanted him to… It was like you just wanted him."

"I'm sorry, Rora— I was never going to do anything, it was just a crush—"

"You had a thing for him growing up, didn't you?"

"Of course I did! He was the brooding quiet guy! Exactly the type I read about, the type of person who would do just about anything for me, who I always hoped I would be with. I'm sorry, Rora, I am… but he was everything for me. He made me think that maybe I wasn't so alone."

"You're not alone. You're never alone, Caleb, not with me. I'm sorry you didn't feel like you could tell me about all of this." Tears trace down my chin and neck, though I don't do anything to stop them. I just hold tight to my brother.

My brother who was always so strong for me, as he breaks down in my arms for the first time.

He was there for me all of my life. Every breakdown, every panic attack, he's been there holding my hand. He's always been there for me, and he's never let me help him back.

I love my brother. I love him more than anything, and I've never been so proud of him in my entire life. I love him.

22

Eric

She doesn't stop me from loading my bags into her

brother's car. She doesn't stop me from getting in the
passenger's seat, from sorting through my passport and tickets.
She doesn't stop me, no matter how much I want her to.

She can't. I know that— that she has to let me leave. That if
she keeps me here, she'll hate herself.

Yet I can't help but wish she'd just… stop me.

~ (~

They're both silent as we drive to the airport together. Her eyes are filled with tears, but I can't reach over and hold her hand like I'd normally want to.

It's over. After everything, it's over. I love her and she loves me, but it doesn't matter because we can't be together anymore. We can't be together no matter how much we want to.

I'm walking away. I promised myself I wouldn't, but I am. I'm walking away from her.

I don't know what heartbreak feels like. Or maybe I do, now. It's a throbbing sort of pain, not like it's shattering— not, that's over too quickly. It's more like a throbbing pain. Every few minutes, it gets better or it gets worse, and there's no way to predict which.

Right now, it's getting worse. The stereo of Caleb's car softly spews Elton John into the air around us, but none of us are paying any attention to it. I love her, and I'm walking away. For a job of all things. A stupid, amazing, ruinous job.

I know she's right, that the second I decided I wanted to turn down the job, I began to resent that she's the only thing that could ever make me willing to do it. She's the only person important enough to me for me to turn down a job like this, and yet she's the one forcing me to do it.

Forcing me to leave her.

The one thing I didn't want to do, I have to. All because she loves me and I love her. I thought it would mean we'd stay together, the fact that we love each other, but instead it's driving us apart. No amount of love or care for each other makes it so we'll stay together now.

I'm leaving, and she's letting me go.

~ (~

She and Caleb walk me through the airport at a slow pace, trying desperately to get just a little bit more time together, but it doesn't work out. We make it to the TSA lines before we'd like to.

I wish I weren't leaving.

It isn't like it is in the movies. She doesn't look back as I ride up an elevator, we don't just miss each other's glances. She doesn't try to run through security to kiss me one last time. I walk through a metal detector and I can't see her anymore, and that's the end of it. She's gone from my sight, but I can still feel her.

It doesn't matter, though, because this is the end of it. This is the end of the line when it comes to her, and I don't have the choice to get back on the train and ride back in time. I wish I had just one more minute with her, the way it was before, but I don't. I can't have her again, I can't go back and redo it all. I don't really want to, either, because as much as I hate to leave her… I have to, and I know it'll turn out well. I know it'll work out.

~ (~

The plane ride to Italy is long, the plane overcrowded with travelers. Each one of them has their own story, their own life to live, though my thoughts are stuck elsewhere. On her. Always on her.

The flight attendant hands me a cup of Coke, leaving behind the can as he goes to check on the next person down the line. The woman who sits beside me shushes her toddler as he ogles the small television in front of him, which seems to be playing some kid's movie from the 90's. I can't focus on that, though. Not when I know that she's probably leaving the airport right now. That Caleb is probably driving her home, or back to the apartment.

Within the span of a year, I've fallen head over heels in love with a girl that I can never, ever truly have. I've broken my own heart, expecting too much from someone who can only give me a small part of her own.

And every night, I stay up thinking about her, and I know that that's what I'm going to spend the rest of my life doing.

This year, I fell in love with Aurora James, my best friend's sister. She's the best thing I've ever been given the chance to have, and I know that I screwed it up.

But every day, I look at that stupid camera she gave me, the little bit of plastic that is at least 100 dollars cheaper than every other camera I own, and it's my favorite. It's easy to forget that I have a million other photographs, because the ones with her in them are the ones I love to look at the most. In fact, they're pretty much the only ones I can stand to look at at the moment.

I got them all developed right before I left, the envelope filled with them sitting in my bag, untouched. It's still sealed shut, I haven't had the courage to open it yet, though I desperately want to.

Or, I guess, I want to see her. That's all I want really, just to see her face as she laughs at something so incredibly stupid.

So yeah. This year, I fell head over heels in love with a girl I was never supposed to fall for. A girl who I knew was looking for a distraction, for a way to feel alive. She could never have loved me the way that I loved her, but through all of our doubts, all of the issues and panicked moments and fearful kisses, all I ever did was love her.

Maybe I wasn't in love with Aurora when I offered up 2 months. I probably wouldn't have done it if I was. I don't think I'm so much of a masochist as to want to break my own heart, but hell if I would know. I think I'd let her cut out my heart if it meant just one more kiss.

~ ☾ ~

Aurora Hope James,

I fell in love with you the moment I met you. We were young, and yet it never mattered to me, because you were my everything. You were the best person in the world to me. My sunshine.

It sounds cheesy, I know, but I couldn't leave without giving you something. I know I've done a lot of things to piss you off in the last few months, but I truly hope this makes up for it in some way. I can never give you enough to make up for everything you've given me, but I think this is at least a start.

This is the last time we'll talk for a while. I know you don't want me calling and texting you from Italy, so I won't. I'll leave you be.

I know I should be asking you to wait for me, but I can't do that. I can't ask you to wait when I know you don't want to. You don't deserve to have to wait on me. So, I'm going to ask you to do the opposite. Move on.

When you're ready to, I hope you bury my things in your closet and you find someone who can make you so incredibly happy, but until then... Remember you're not alone. You're never alone.

I love you so much, Aurora. I love you like I've never loved anyone else.

And I'm asking you to— when it's time —forget me and move on.

Goodbye, Aurora.

Love,
E.M.

23

Aurora

I suppose that it was all for the best that he didn't really come back for me. I don't know what I would have done if he had.

Eric was, in many ways, the best and worst thing that ever happened to me. He loved me more than anything, and I loved him too, but we still broke each other. Sometimes I think he took a part of me with him when he left for Italy.

I haven't seen him in two years. I've finally stopped counting the time.

Maybe I still love him. Maybe I don't. I honestly don't know if what we had was love at all, but I don't mind anyway.

I found my one true love in the pages of a book. A book I created from ink, with the keys on my laptop. I wove the pages of a universe together with my hands. I did something meaningful.

No one can forget you when you've left something behind.

I guess it's a good thing we broke up when we did. We were never going to work out the way we hoped we would.

But somehow, I can't help but think that he was one of the best things that ever happened to me. That he changed my life in some incredible unforeseen way. That when he told me he got that job, I should have told him it was okay— that maybe we could make it work or something.

That I still loved him.

Maybe we'll meet again in another life, or maybe we won't. Maybe he'll come back to me and maybe he won't.

Maybe I'll never see him again. But even so, even knowing that the person I love more than I love myself may never come back, I'm still happy I was with him for the time I was. I never used to believe in soulmates. I still don't, but I know one thing for sure.

He was my very own old soul. He was mine and I was his, and that's what really matters. No single cigarette or pair of large tortoise shell glasses or matchstick or cup of tainted Dr. Pepper could ever change that fact— I was his and he was mine, and that was more than enough for the both of us.

Although I won't lie, I do hope my own characters can find their way through their messes better than we did. In some ways, I wonder if Eric will ever know the effect he once had on me. If he'll know that he inspired my greatest achievement, or hell, if he'll even read it. I wonder if he'll recognize the arguments as ours or how every kiss is modeled off of our own. I wonder if he'll remember them the way I do. I wonder if he still has the photos and the camera or if he even remembers them.

I suppose it isn't up to me either way. If he does or if he doesn't. I remember him and that's all that matters to me anyways. I remember our love like the strike of a match on a concrete barrier in the smoking area of a dingy hotel off I-40 East. I remember our love like the embers falling from a cigarette. We were a beautiful flaming mess until we crumbled.

We were beautiful.

The End.

...or maybe it's just the beginning...

What Now?

An excerpt from *Within the Matchsticks* by Aurora Hope James.

Dedicated to my own fleeting flame, my first love.

Once, when I was young, I asked my brother what it was like to be loved.

His answer?

It feels like the moon and sun are shining in the same sky. Always different, but equal. Symbiotic, living and loving one another in that moment. It feels like a fire which will be quick to burn out, but the warmth is there and it's a warmth you'll always remember, no matter what happens.

The issue with this, though, is that when you think of the sun and the moon, they rarely live in the same sky, and when you think of a match, you remember that it will always burn out—

you remember that the fire will recede down the wood and burn your fingers and turn the tips of them red before you have to drop it or put it out. The sun and the moon are never equals and the match will always go out in the end, but we still watch for those times when it doesn't. We use lighters because they don't burn out on our fingertips and we long for the summer when the days are longer and there are those few minutes when you can see the moon fighting for its presence in the daylight.

And with all of the great love stories we read, perhaps the idea of a one in a million love seems idiotic, even ironic, but not to them.

Not to Delilah Green and not to Jace Marcus. Not to the two misfits in love, unthought of and unliked by everyone around them. Everyone but each other.

Because just once, the sun and the moon shone together for them, equals in the sky, and the matchstick never went out. No burnt fingers or broken hearts could get in their way. They were together, fully and completely together and they loved it.

For once, they were completely each other's.

And even now, as ghosts in that same small town, they're together, their relationship forever imprinted on every square inch. Their shadows dance together on the walls of the old boutiques and antique shops as if in the light of a hundred matchsticks.

That is their love. That is the flaming story of Delilah and Jace.

And god was their story amazing while it lasted.

Acknowledgements

I would like to thank my family for all that they have done to
help me succeed and make it as far as I have— both in life and in
my writing. A huge thanks to them: my parents, for the lifetime
of support they have given me and the work they have done to
hold my hand and help me through life. I would like to thank my
mom, Jackie, for inspiring me to write this book with the
hundreds of stories she's told me over the years and the books
she's bought me (she says I have too many now but I
wholeheartedly disagree). I would like to thank my dad, Nathan,
for making me believe that I was capable of writing and
publishing my own novel. I would like to thank my little sister,
Chloe, for giving me the courage to be creative no matter what. I
would like to thank my best friends, who stood with me while I
went through the ups and downs of writing and who celebrated
and mourned with me through the highs and the lows. Who sat

with me constantly and gave me the encouragement I needed to go through with publishing. Even now, as I write these acknowledgements, I'm sitting with them, and I could not be more grateful to be here. Even though we will be going our separate ways soon, I know that each and every one of them will be amazingly successful and I can't wait to see what they all end up doing. They are some of the smartest people I know, and I believe that having them as friends has made me a smarter and kinder person than I was before.

To my camping family, who have spent many years inspiring me to be creative and who have acted as my chosen family all my life. If I didn't have you all, I don't know what I would do, but I know I certainly wouldn't have had the drive or courage to write this novel.

Most importantly, I would like to thank the people who had a direct hand in publishing this novel. To those who read and helped me to improve my novel to make it what it is today, I am eternally grateful for your help and friendship. I am so incredibly happy to know you all and I am so thankful for the help and support you gave me. To my mom and dad, who picked through my novel carefully and helped me to edit it. To my sister, who used her many artistic talents to make me an incredible cover. To J, who was the first person to ask to read my novel, and who gave me the most thoughtful feedback imaginable, who allowed me to understand my own characters more than I originally thought I could, and who helped me through some of the times when I thought I couldn't do it. To Nova, who as a writer herself has given me so much advice and who has told me so much of her own stories. To Alex, who was the first person to read my book all the way through besides myself (he finished it in two hours flat) and who gave me so much encouragement along the way. To Emma, who asked me to write a second book so that she could know what happens to Aurora and Eric, but who understood my hesitation to do so. And to Sophia, who is one of the kindest people I know, who despite being so incredibly busy offered to read my book in her free time. Thank you all so much, I could not have done this without you. I am forever grateful for the support, love and kindness you all have shown me.

About the Author

Ella Marshall is a 17-year old author from Hillsborough, North Carolina. She was born and raised in the small town she calls home and her book definitely reflects that love of her community. She's a uniquely independent and intellectual person, and she was raised by some of the greatest people in the world. Her first novel, We Are The Old Souls, is inspired by her family— and not only the one she was born with. Speaking with Ella, you'll realize that a lot of her life has been surrounded by what she calls her "Camping family". These are some of the most important people in her life, and she loves them more than anything. They inspired her novel more than anything else. They're her very own group of Old Souls.

Ella grew up reading Young Adult fiction. From the time she was ten, she was enjoying these novels, and it's inspired her to write one of her own. As she puts it, she has the "ability to create a world." and she takes that very seriously. The novel she's written is a clear representation of that ability. It's a world which she's molded to fit her own ideas, and one which represents the love she feels for her own world.